Date: 6/4/20

LP FIC SEXTON
Sexton, Margaret Wilkerson,
The revisioners

THE REVISIONERS

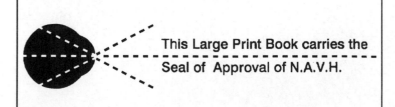

This Large Print Book carries the
Seal of Approval of N.A.V.H.

THE REVISIONERS

MARGARET WILKERSON SEXTON

THORNDIKE PRESS
A part of Gale, a Cengage Company

Thorndike Press® Large Print African-American.
The text of this Large Print edition is unabridged.
Other aspects of the book may vary from the original edition.
Set in 16 pt. Plantin.

LIBRARY OF CONGRESS CIP DATA ON FILE.
CATALOGUING IN PUBLICATION FOR THIS BOOK
IS AVAILABLE FROM THE LIBRARY OF CONGRESS

ISBN-13: 978-1-4328-7671-5 (hardcover alk. paper)

Published in 2020 by arrangement with Counterpoint Press, LLC.

Printed in Mexico
Print Number: 01   Print Year: 2020

For my ancestors, especially my father

I go forth alone, and stand as ten thousand.

MAYA ANGELOU

AVA

It was King who told me we forgot the photograph. Twelve years old, but he'd been washing his own clothes since he was eight, and was often the one to remind me to take the trash out on Thursdays. I didn't intend to place all that responsibility on him — he was a child — but he identified the holes in my capacity and dove into them. While I was filing motions for Mr. Jeff at Wilkerson & Associates, he was microwaving neat squares of beef lasagna. And now this, the picture my grandmother's great-grandmother had had taken of herself, standing at the edge of her farm. Miss Josephine. Her husband had just died, and you could not miss that in her eyes, the loneliness. But you could also glimpse the pride: the rows of corn, their stalks double her height, the chickens at her feet. A smokehouse with shingles planked toward

9

the roof like two hands in prayer.

"We could go back and get it," King says.

I shake my head. "It's too late," I say, and maybe it is and maybe it isn't, but I'm afraid if I turn back, I won't make it through the stained-glass doors of the uptown mansion in front of us. I hadn't fully come to the decision to move here, more like the decision had wound its way through me, and if I had another hour, another drive east, I might just stay over on that side of town, where my mama would welcome me. But I was tired of disappointing her. She was hard on me when I was a child. She held so much promise when she'd met my father at Tulane. She was one of the only blacks on campus and she caught his eye though the only black woman he'd known was his housekeeper, Mary. Six months later, my mother was pregnant. My father went on to law school. She had planned on going too but it would have been difficult for her without a baby; with me, it was nearly impossible. Still she did it, all the while working odd jobs as a waitress, caretaker, stenographer. My father felt neglected and took up with a woman from his Civil Procedure study group. My mother said she was better off without him, but for a long time when she looked at me, when she answered

10

my questions, when she tucked me in to sleep at night, I could sense her bitterness straining through her tight smiles.

"We better go in," I say. "It's getting dark," and King lets out a tired sigh.

"Why can't we just go to Maw Maw's?" he asks. He's been asking this all week and I repeat again what I've been saying.

"This is a good opportunity for us, King. A better school. We'll see each other more 'cause you'll just be downstairs."

"Yeah, but living in this old lady's house. This old white lady." He pauses. "It's weird."

"No weirder than living with Maw Maw that one time. Probably better because she won't be all up in our business. Plus this house is huge. Grandma Martha will have her wing, we'll have ours. You probably won't even see her."

He sucks his teeth but he shifts in his seat and grips the handle of his backpack.

When I open my car door, he opens his too. We didn't pack a whole lot. Our furniture is in storage, and otherwise we don't own much more than our clothes, one lamp, some framed pictures of me and my mother when I was a child, me clinging to her waist like any minute someone might snatch her. We gather the little we can hold and walk

11

up the long brick walkway, past the two-tiered angel fountain in the courtyard, through the iron lace gate. I use my key to open up and Grandma Martha isn't at the door to greet us, but she's already told me where we'll stay and I know my way to the second floor. Her room is just beyond us on the third. King has never been inside and his mouth is open as he sizes it up, the grand crystal chandelier, the red uphol-stered chairs, the Oriental rugs over the mahogany floors, the paintings of her ances-tors, their thin lips pressed together.

In his room, he sets his backpack down. Just to the side of his four-poster bed, a window looks out to the driveway where our beat-up white Camry seems out of place. The bed is the height of his waist. I remem-ber at our apartment, he'd flop on his old one after school and here he has to climb on top.

"I told you the house was big," I say.

"Too big," he says back. "Too nice. I don't even feel comfortable touching anything."

I almost tell him he's right, that he shouldn't touch a thing, but I want him to feel at home here.

"You're careful enough," I say.

I hear a voice behind me.

"You don't need to worry about this old

stuff." Grandma Martha. I turn to greet her. And she is how she always is: bracelets clanging and perfume wafting and ironed white button-down shirt and colored pants and smart sandals with her toes painted a mild shade of pink. She is seventy-eight and her wrinkles are fine; her hair clings to her scalp before it's clipped at the base of her head into a winding bun. But I can still glimpse who she was when I graduated from college, when she wore a cream St. John suit with a matching hat, and even when I was four and she fed me squares of baker's chocolate on the balcony, not too sweet because I wouldn't want to lose my waistline.

"Oh," I say, and a shot of relief flows through me because she has that way of putting me at ease. We didn't see each other much growing up. My daddy went on to have a gang of blond-haired children and I'd only know their ages through the Christmas cards each year. Still Grandma Martha sought me out every summer, offered to pay for tennis and math and science camps. She'd arrange for my mother to drop me at her house, and there'd be a frilly Janie and Jack dress in my size waiting on the daybed in the guest room. I'd change into it, then we'd drive her olive-green Mercedes to lunch at Mr. B's in the Quarter. For holidays, she'd mail me envelopes addressed to Miss Ava Jackson with a crisp $100 bill and pink barrettes enclosed. Anytime I'd meet her, my mother would preach on the way over, remind me of what I already knew: not to put my elbows on the table, to take slow, small bites, to say *Yes ma'am,* to never force my grandmother's hand, and I obliged even though I knew Grandma didn't care about that stuff. I told my mother that, but she never responded.

Once Grandma's husband passed, the attention ramped up — Grandma bought prom dresses and makeup tutorials at Lakeside's Stila counter. And when I had King, and my own husband started to drift, she'd watch the baby for me while I slept or got my nails done. She'd sit on the sofa in my modest two-bedroom and fold his onesies like she hadn't had a housekeeper her entire life. Now she has more, a chef named Binh, a part-time nurse named Juanita, who even walks her up and down the streetcar tracks when the weather permits. Still, she'd called me one Saturday crying. She was lonely. I'd settled her down, then I'd confessed I wasn't faring much better, laid off from my paralegal job, and she'd proposed I move in. A win-win, she'd said. A win-win, though at seventy-eight, she is not who she has been. She walks with a limp; she wears Depends and not just at night, but she's always seemed mentally sound. She dresses and feeds herself, and she still has that softness to her that makes me want to tell her my secrets. She still makes me feel welcome here, and finally, like I made the right decision.

She reaches for King.

"It's so good to have you," she says, and she pulls him into her. I can see him still clenched up in his back, but he is polite like I've taught him and he thanks her.

"No, thank you," she says. "I haven't had children with me for I don't know how long. It's welcome, I can tell you. It will lighten up the place."

"And you, my granddaughter," she reaches out for me next. It is nice to hear her call me that, granddaughter. Growing up, I don't think I ever heard her acknowledge the bloodline. The omission didn't occur to me until I was older, but once I noticed it, I started offering her subtle chances to say aloud what we were to each other, but she wouldn't.

"I can't tell you how much it means to me that you would uproot your life like this," she says now.

I don't bother to say we didn't have that many other options. I could have gone to my mother's, sure, but there was her mouth to consider, and I couldn't bear the cost. Besides, where would it land us? In a year's time I'd still be in the same predicament. Grandma Martha on the other hand offered to pay me my other salary just to sit with her during the day. King will start tomorrow at the best public middle school in New Orleans. At the end of the year, I'd have enough for my own place, maybe just a townhome and probably one in the hood at that, but still, we could lay down some roots. I made good money with Mr. Jeff, and I got my bartending license to supplement once King's daddy left, but I had to drag myself into Vincent's every night, then back to Mr. Jeff's in the morning. I'm not stupid, I know I should be grateful to have had a job at all, but from where I'm standing, with the antique writing table at my hip, and the signed oil paintings on the walls above me, it might be okay to start to ask for more.

"Well, I'll leave you two to settle in," Grandma says, and she hobbles off down the stairs, taking longer on each one than I remember.

She turns back and catches me looking.

"Maybe I'll see you for dinner. Of course we don't have to sit down every night, but since it's our first one together, we'll want to commemorate it, won't we?"

I look at King the same time he looks at me. We had heard stories about the chef, whom Grandma has always called Bee-Bee, about the made-to-order meals, bread pudding, pastries with chocolate ganache. He smiles.

"That'll be lovely," I say.

I get up with Binh before dinner to tour the bar. As much as I complained about the schedule, I miss my bartending days, and out of respect, I still make a cocktail every night, pour a little bit out for my former self. Tonight it's a gin and tonic, two parts gin, five parts tonic. I chill the glasses, then add the ice, pour the gin over the large cubes, squeeze the first lime before the tonic hits; the second lime is just the cherry on top really. I lean against the counter, take a sip, and set the glass down. It's perfect.

Binh serves fried chicken and waffles with a side of sweet potato biscuits and rosemary jam. I'm supposed to be on a plan, but I have a weakness for breakfast food. I reach for two waffles and a biscuit, and I'm not shy with the syrup either. King eyes his plate

17

with suspicion, Grandma's old wedding china.

"I thought this menu might be more modern," Grandma says, pleased with herself. She watches King eat with what seems to be fascination. He's wearing his uniform: a Nike hoodie and athletic shorts with basketball tights underneath. At twelve, he is a head taller than I am, a chocolate boy with dredlocks that touch his shoulders. I married his father because I couldn't deny the first boy who called me when he said he would, who told me he loved me before I fell asleep at night, but if I'm honest, there were other things. King's daddy couldn't have been blacker, and I was still lamenting my light skin, my checked-out father at the root of it. Even the Seventh Ward girls at school read oppressor in my face. I was a heavy child, still do shop in the plus-size section of most stores; I have more hair than most families combined, and I wear it out in a curly brown fro that almost touches my shoulders. It's the style now, but it wasn't back then. My mama didn't let me straighten it, and the unoriginal children would call me Chia Pet and Free Willy, or sing *He's got jungle fever, she's got jungle fever* when I walked into the room. And my plan worked; nobody would look at King

18

and not know he was a black child. Not only that, he's cool in a way I never showed. When I'd pick him up from McMain, a posse would escort him to my car, but it had started to be more than the middle schoolers. It was the high schoolers as well, some of whom I recognized from the street corners.

Now he picks at his food.

I know what he's thinking. *White people know they don't have no business serving fried chicken.*

"Please stick to the rivers and the lakes that you're used to," he sings from the old-school music I listen to on FM98 sometimes, and I reprimand him though I want to laugh. Grandma Martha stops me.

"Let him be a child," she says. "You only have a few more years of it left. You better enjoy it because then they're old and" — she gestures around the long table — "well, you're left by your lonesome," she finishes.

"You have us," I whisper.

"Oh, sure," she says. "I only meant, when I bought this table, I imagined I'd have my children around it forever, surrounding me, into my old age, but —" her face loosens and drags and then she picks it back up in a flash. "But here's to new connections." She lifts her glass of soda water, and I lift the gin and tonic I crafted, and King lifts his chocolate milk, and we clink them all together and I catch him smiling.

That night as I'm turning down her bed, Grandma Martha asks me to sit on the wicker bedroom bench across from her.

"This is so nice." She extends her legs and pulls them back in in soft motions. She's taken her medical alert system off and placed it on her dresser.

"Yeah, I mean your house is out of this world," I say. The bedroom is immaculate, and about the size of my old apartment. There's a cream-colored chaise lounge in the corner, a fireplace with a white marble mantel, a gold-framed mirror to my left.

"I'm not talking about that," she says. "I'm talking about you." She dips her hand down toward the room where King is staying. "The family. The life you built. King is so cared for, he's so happy. I tried to do that with your dad, but I don't think I got it right. I spoiled him is the thing," she goes on. "He never had to work for anything, and look where it got him; I only hear from him every few months, and even then it's just a five-minute call. Every year it's a different woman. I never thought your mother was the right one, but . . ." she trails off, then starts right back up again, "at least

20

there was you to care for."

"I'm sorry I wasn't around more, when you were growing up. You needed that influence, but I was trying to be a good wife. I was too caught up with the times. You know things were so different back then, but the child, the child just needs love. The child doesn't see color, that's what I'd always tell your grandfather but he couldn't grasp it."

If she wants forgiveness, I'm not ready to extend it, and I don't say a word. I'm here though, and that's something.

"And your father," she goes on. "I never told anyone this, there was such a stigma around infertility back then, but it took me years to conceive him. It was terrible, heart-wrenching, almost wrecked my marriage from the inside out. I thought we wouldn't make it through, but then, I came out with this perfect little baby." She shakes her head at the memory. "That's why I clung to him so."

"Anyway," she scrunches her face up in delight, "when I was a little girl, we'd run through the fields at night with our gentlemen callers, slip our hands in theirs. They'd try for second base, and we'd allow it, but we'd make them fight. Everybody looked up to Daddy. Even men his own age didn't call him by his first name. Mr. Dufrene, they said. And the boys, well, they all wanted to be seen with a Dufrene girl." She smiles. "All of them," she repeats. "They'd start sniffing around once we turned thirteen, and after that we were never alone."

I had brought the dinner's gin and tonic upstairs with me, and I'm grateful for that decision now. I take a few sips; I wasn't prepared for the stroll down memory lane is all.

She points to her jewelry box, and I lean over toward her bureau and pass it to her. She lifts a diamond necklace from it.

"You like this?" she asks.

"Very much," I say. My mama had found religion in her New Age church and since then she'd say we had different strains of ourselves in the universe, like there was me here sitting with Grandma Martha, but there was the other version of myself who had finished college in four years, not seven, who didn't eat mint chocolate chip ice cream at night, who married the right man, or at least divorced King's daddy sooner. There was the version of myself who knew how beautiful I was, how smart, how kind. A version of myself who didn't need an alarm clock because she had ambition ringing through her bones, and that woman attended balls where she wore that diamond

22

necklace.

"It's yours," Grandma Martha says now.

"No, no way in the world," I say shaking my head. "I could never. That's not what this is," I add just to be clear.

She stretches her cheeks in a quiet smile. "I was going to give it to you anyway. It will look so nice against your beautiful brown skin, and the other grandchildren, well, they don't deserve the pot I piss in to be frank."

I laugh. "But Grandma Martha, I saw the photo of you at your husband's, at Grandfather's, swearing in," I correct myself. "You wore it then and it was beautiful. You might want to remember it that way."

She shakes her head. "There will be a time coming real soon when I'll be beneath the dirt and you'll be above it, and there's no jewelry in the world that's going to spring me back up again, now is there?"

I don't know what to say to that. She talks like this sometimes and I don't like it. I hadn't grown up with her but I am getting used to leaning on her, more and more each year.

"All right, Grandma." I stand and kiss her cheek. "I'm just a floor away."

I turn down her lights.

I check in on King on my way to my own room.

He's unpacking his shirts, hanging them in the closet, but he looks like he's been crying.

I pull him toward the bed and sit down beside him.

"It's going to be all right," I say.

"No, it's not," he says, twisting his dreadlocks in a frenzy like he does when he's concentrating or nervous, or sad. "I'm telling you, I have a bad feeling about this house. Didn't you feel it when you walked in? It's like walking into a refrigerator and shutting the door behind you." He starts to whisper. "I have a bad feeling about her." He nods in Grandma's direction.

"About your great-grandmother?" I ask. "She's family."

"Not all kinfolk is skinfolk," he says.

I laugh at that. "Boy, it's supposed to be the other way around."

"Nah, think about it, Mama."

"Look," I say. "Give it a month? If you don't like it after that, we can figure out our next steps."

He pauses.

"Fine, Mama," he says.

He's back to fiddling with his iPhone, and before I stand, sound bursts out. It's that new Childish Gambino song he bumps. He doesn't let me kiss him too long and then he's laying his Nikes and Pumas out in the closet just so.

"We're going to be okay here," I say, but he doesn't hear me, and the lyrics follow me out his door.

Too late
You wanna make it right, but now it's too
   late

I set up the lamp I brought outside King's room. It is a classic trophy lamp with a brass finish and a black shade. King would never say he's afraid of the dark, but I know it soothes him to see an outline of the familiar when he wakes up before morning. I switch the light on, then go to my room, sink into my bed. The mattress is thicker and softer than what I'm used to. I've been running on adrenaline since I made the decision. Grandma had been looking for a companion for some time and I'd contacted Traveling Angels for her but then King's school called; he had been in a fight. I'd driven straight over, and sure enough there he was with his eye already swelling, holding a blood-soaked napkin to his nose.

"You should see the other kid," he'd joked, but I'd gone off on him.

"You know we don't do that," I said. "You

know we don't."

And he'd tried to explain. This boy from the ninth grade was messing with his friend Nathan. He didn't have a choice but to defend him. Wasn't I always telling him to stand up for what he believed in? Well, he believed in his friend.

I'd told him I wasn't raising a thug, but that night while he ate stuffed mirliton with garlic bread, his favorite, I watched him, my son whose newborn face I could still envision, and I wondered where I'd gone wrong. We had lived in a house when he was born. A modest one a few blocks south of Freret, and a policeman lived on one side of us, and a secretary lived on the other. Then King's daddy left, and the rent inched up every month, first $30, then $100, and Mr. Jeff was a good man, but he couldn't clone my paycheck. When it was time to move elsewhere, there was nowhere to go. Five years after Katrina, my neighborhood had bloomed. We had a white mayor and fancy restaurants that stretched a dozen blocks, but all I could afford was a redeveloped unit in what used to be the projects. With the neat lawns and fresh paint, you'd never know what the apartment had been, but the D-boys on the corner told on it, and I'd said to King that I wasn't raising no thug,

26

but I wondered at that moment if that wasn't exactly who I was raising. I called Grandma and I told her she didn't need to look anymore, that the companion would be me.

Tonight I'm walking distance from where I'd been but it might as well be a world away. Except for the security van that passes on the hour, there's little traffic, and the crickets and the occasional wind chime are the only breaks in silence. I'm still tipsy from my drink, and I hit up Spotify for Sam Smith, set up a song for repeat. It was Byron's favorite, mine too, and I don't miss him, as much as I miss the fullness I felt being part of a unit, the depth and the purpose.

You say I'm crazy
'Cause you don't think I know what
    you've done

It doesn't take long to fall asleep but I wake up soon after, my right foot shooting forward as if in the other world I'd been running. I close my eyes, and a thread of the scene is back. My legs were pumping through water, clear enough to drink, but it smelled like rot. There was the thunder of horses galloping behind me, and out of their mouths streamed sentences I couldn't grasp. King was with me, but he was a grown man with a different face, and just before I opened my eyes, I heard a shot ring out, and someone scream.

Grandma pulled some strings to get King into her neighborhood public school, and he's nervous in the morning, wondering about his old friends, and barely eating the grits and eggs Binh prepared. I try to remind him of the positive ways the new school will be different, but he doesn't say a word all the way through the carpool line.

He had told me he was afraid he'd be the only black kid in his class, and his worry wasn't far off. There are a few sprinkled into the larger student body. Their mothers roll up in Porsches and Benzes; I can see from the car windows that the women are wearing suits, and they smile at me but they are fast smiles. I am not their own. But I'm okay with that because there are STEM classes at this place that you don't have to pay for, a jazz band, a student-run literary magazine. King writes poems at night and sometimes I see them scribbled out on the dresser.

Baby-love ones, though he's never had a girlfriend: *you be my earth, and I'll be your moon,* and I'm not saying he's Langston Hughes, but everybody's got to start somewhere.

It's just a minimum day today, and King is buzzing when I pick him up. At dinner, he talks with his mouth full, but he's so excited I allow it. There's an assembly in the morning, he says, where kids give a speech about anything that's bothering them. He got up and talked about moving to a new school.

"Afterward all these kids walked up to me in the hallways and introduced themselves. At my old school, somebody would have called me a punk, but here they were so" — he pauses — "nice."

Grandma Martha is beaming.

"And that's just the beginning," she says. "You're going to meet so many friends at this new school. Fine kids who will be good influences for you."

His face suddenly turns, and he sets his fork down.

"I had friends at my old school too," he says.

"Yes, yes, of course you did, but I'm just saying . . ." her voice trails off.

"We're both just so happy you had a good

30

day," I say, and he seems to relax.

Spaghetti is one of his favorite foods, and he cleans the plate, then asks to be excused.

I clear the table, then help Grandma upstairs. I hadn't noticed her outfit when she was sitting, the same classic button-down shirt with starched white pants that she always chooses, but she's spilled tomato sauce from dinner and didn't bother to wipe it. Even now, the red juice is running down the pant crease. Then too, there is an odor that wafts up from her, the unmistakable scent of funk. I almost ask if she needs help cleaning, but I see her heading into her bathroom, and I let it go.

King is sitting on the edge of his bed when I walk by his room. I go in and sit down next to him, rub the back of his neck like I've done since he was a baby at my breast. Sometimes he allows it, and sometimes he doesn't. Today he sinks into me.

"What is it?" I ask. "You seem like you got a little down back there."

"I don't know. Just the way she said that thing about these kids being good influences. Like my friends weren't good."

"I hear you. I noticed that too," I say. "But you have to understand she didn't mean it that way. She's getting old and she can't

31

always find the right words, but trust me. If anybody knows those are good kids, it's her."

He doesn't say anything.

"You miss your friends, don't you, buddy?" I ask.

He nods.

"How 'bout this? I'm off this weekend. We could go back to the old neighborhood. I'll call Senait, we'll set up something with her and Nathan and Issa, sound good?"

He nods.

"I love you, Mom," he says.

"I love you more," I say back.

Midsentence I hear a crash from just beyond the door and I rush to the landing.

Grandma is standing outside King's bedroom. I gasp. I don't mean to but I didn't expect to see her there; not only that, her hair is never down the way it is now, and I see for the first time that it reaches her stomach. She has changed already, and her nightgown is pale and translucent; dark and light flashes of her naked body shine through. I look away.

"What happened?" I ask, my eyes darting behind her.

"Oh, this lamp just fell down. I swear I didn't even touch it, just passed next to it, and it leapt to the floor."

32

"Oh," I say. It's my mother's great-great-grandmother's lamp, the only thing of Josephine's that we own. I don't need to examine it to see the brass is chipped.

"I'm so sorry," Grandma says. "I can have Juanita run out tomorrow and get you another one. I've seen this very thing in Nordstrom."

"No, Grandma, that's all right. Don't worry about it. You just surprised me is all. I'll walk you back to bed."

Along the way to her room, she wants to discuss each picture we pass.

"That one is my wedding day," she says, pointing to a black-and-white eight-by-ten. "He got the jewel. All the boys in the county would wait for us by the farm entrance."

"Oh, and I see why," I say back, not unlike the way I might respond to a toddler.

We keep walking. When we reach the room, I watch her navigate to her bed, wait to hear her mattress creak under her. She must know I'm still there because she talks the whole while, her back to me, first about the weather and then as the bed shifts, so does the topic.

"I hope you're not thinking about leaving," she says in a near whisper. I almost think I've misheard her.

"Oh? Of course not, Grandma. We just

got here. Where would I go?"

She sighs. "People have their places. Their dreams. That I know. It always seems more pleasant in somebody else's fields. But we're good to you here, right?"

It is an odd question, but I am still thinking about that lamp.

"The very best, Grandma," I say.

"Good. I love you, Ava."

"I love you too, Grandma."

JOSEPHINE

1924

There was no question I would choose the Hampshire — he was already seven hundred pounds, fat off sweet potatoes, milk, beets, and turnips. This last week though I'd cleaned him out with corn because it wasn't every day your only son got married. There would have to be enough pork to feed the parish.

At Wildwood, babies weren't swaddled in white and dipped in water as soon as their color came in, and a man and his woman didn't jump over a broom with their mother's blessing. Once, an aunt who wasn't really my mother's sister fell hard for a man across the swamps. Tom, who didn't like to be called Master, said yes, of course, and they slept in the same cabin that night. Besides that, no attention was paid, and though we settled Resurrection in the West Alexander Parish of Southeast Louisiana

35

over thirty years ago, I still wake up every morning in disbelief. My gratitude is not close to wringing itself out, and out of thanksgiving, I make sure to do everything Tom, who made sure we called him by his first name, wouldn't have done. I bore and raised three children but only one of them is with me now, a son, and for him to choose a bride. Don't get me started.

And the Hampshire is the richest swine. My husband and I started out as sharecroppers on the edge of a bluff that toed the line between Mr. Dennis's farm and the Mississippi River marshes. At first we didn't fare much better here than Wildwood. We'd wake every morning before the sun rose to ride the mule to work on a dirt road straight along the water's edge. But Mr. Dennis was a gambling man, a man who swallowed whiskey straight, and it was only so long before what he had was ours, three hundred acres of cotton, corn, cane, hogs, and cattle. His workers became our workers but we didn't think of them that way. We divided the acres into tracts and parceled them out. We became a community together: we built a church, inside that a school, then a gristmill, a cane mill, a cotton gin that ground corn too. And if we had shingles, everybody had shingles; the same went for our milk cows, and fields to garden. Now that I'm old, my people's hands are my hands. I say that to say things have changed, and it won't fall on me to aim the rifle right between the pig's eyes; to hang it, slit its throat, wash it, skin it, gut it clean. I have someone to do that for me now but I'll still make the decision, point to the black boar with the white belt around the middle, because it has to be the finest.

The door swings open, and I know it is Jericho. With his long stride he runs the way other folk walk, the way I have started to hobble, hunchbacked, but I steady myself to receive him in my arms. He is a red boy, just like his daddy, and just like my husband, and his head, hair cut tight to his scalp, reaches my waist.

"You smell like outside," I say, examining his dusty blue overalls. There's a hole in the knee I would have to patch up that evening.

"I've been playing, Grandma."

"Hmph. Well, it's a bath for you tonight."

He doesn't say a word.

"You know what I mean, don't you?"

He still doesn't speak. Then, "What if I don't want them to marry?"

I tap him more than slap him, right on his shoulder.

"Lord, deliver me. We're grateful for

Eliza," I say like I'm reciting my morning psalm. "She's kind to you, she knows her letters, she could probably learn you some better than that teacher we pay. She'll take good care of Major and you too."

He pauses, sits down, takes off his wide-brimmed hat, and taps his fingers against the hickory table. I can smell the lilies in a jar in the center. I get up on instinct and I pour him some cool lemonade. I still find new mercy in the fact this house belongs to me; that the pine boards overlap to keep the rodents out; the windows swing all the way open. There's three bedrooms, one so large I can fit two beds side by side; I have an icebox instead of ceramic barrels, and I won't ever run out of sacks of flour or my shelves of preserved raspberries and canned tomatoes, not if I live for ten more years, which I won't. I watch Jericho drinking like his lips are a miracle to behold. Surely my own children drank lemonade. Surely they ran in and called for me over any other, but I don't remember it. I don't.

"*Will* she take care of me?" he sets his glass down. "I ain't her child. Pretty soon she'll start having her own and I'll start smelling like fried skunk."

"What do you know about fried skunk?" I

shake my head but I understand his meaning.

"It's from one of your stories," he says, "the one about you escaping, when you were hiding in the swamps."

"Nah, we didn't eat no skunks; rabbit, coons, squirrels, possum stew with sweet potatoes, but no skunks, young man. Anyway, that's enough of that," I say because it is one thing to dip into the past but to be hauled up and tossed back in it, don't get me started. Otherwise I don't know what to tell him. "You been praying like I taught you?"

"Yes, ma'am."

"Add your worry to the list. I can tell you this: I asked for your daddy to find someone who would love him and love you and who would replace me when I'm gone."

"Don't do that."

"Don't do what? The only thing you can count on is the cycle of life. Anyway, she came in and I believe it's God's doing."

"How do you know though?"

I pause. "I don't. But I will say that I had a dream the night before he brought her home and there was a woman wearing yellow in it, walking through a tunnel waving, and when Eliza walked in, didn't she have a daffodil in her hair?"

"I don't remember."

"She did. So cheer up. Go in the back and get clean; I've got to make these cakes; if you listen, I'll fill one of them with that blueberry jam you like."

He heeds, but I can tell when my words don't take root. Either way, I head out to the garden with its tomatoes, greens and okra, the banks of beets, sweet potatoes and cabbage, and rows of crowder peas, woven through the corn. The yard chickens scatter throughout for seeds and insects. I pass the smokehouse, the well, then the pen, fenced in with zigzag rails. The best hog looks at me with begging eyes, but I point my gnarled finger at him anyway.

We pile as many into the church as we can fit and still the doorway is jammed with witnesses. I sit in the first row of course. Jericho walks in next, his maple-wood skin shining in his dark blue suit, his head held high, till he slinks in right beside me. Next is a little girl whose father works the fields, reaching into a basket and sprinkling gardenias at her feet.

The organist presses down on the pedals, and we stand. Eliza might as well tiptoe into the church from the back. Her yellow skin is powdered smooth, and there's a crown of daffodils woven into her curly bun. I could pick her up with one hand she seems so light, and she sails more than steps down the aisle. The crowd isn't faking when they ooh and aah. They probably haven't seen a bride so lovely, probably won't again. I glance over at her side of the church. Jericho saw them headed in and said without meaning to, "Mama, those folks sho is dignified." I know they are. Her mother, Cyrile, is a schoolteacher at West Alexander Colored Convent School, one of the first schools for blacks in the parish. She sits next to her son, Eliza's brother Louis. People tell me he is hotheaded, and I can sense it, that his pale skin is quick to redden, and he fidgets, picking at his fingers even as his sister's and Major's hands join. Still his suit is hemmed so fine you can scarcely see the edge of his socks. I don't like to compare people. It is like slamming God for making petunias *and* roses, but it doesn't escape me I was born a slave. I can read some, and I made sure Major finished the fourth grade. But he works the farm now, and Eliza's family lives at the intersection of General and Christie Roads. They come from the likes of the Doucets and the Chevaliers. And they have been free for as long as they care to remember.

I remind myself I had a dress made for this event, a pastel yellow silk crepe one with a drop waist and a bowtie at the neck, from a store so fancy I had to pay a white woman to make the purchase. I am a heavy woman — even now, the seams of this gown are straining against my sides — but I know I look good. Once I overheard a younger man say as I was leaving the sick and shut-in ministry prayer meeting, "That Josephine could be my mama but she lookin more like a sister."

Now Jericho's old preschool teacher stands and walks toward the pulpit, clears her throat, passes a look to the organist. The music starts, and the teacher is unsteady when she joins in,

> Three gates in the east
> Three gates in the west
> Three gates in the north
> Three gates in the south
> That makes twelve gates to the city
>   Hallelujah

But it doesn't take long before the song rises from her gut.

Oh, what a beautiful city
Oh, what a beautiful city
Oh, what a beautiful city

And I might as well be standing up there
with her, patting my hand at my side:

There's twelve gates to the city Hallelujah
Walk right in, you're welcome to the city
Step right up welcome to the city
Walk right through those gates to the city
There are twelve gates to the city
    Hallelujah

When the applause settles, the preacher
rises from his chair on the pulpit, walks
toward us, his voice bellowing even at the
start:
    "How many people in a marriage, mem-
bers?"
    "Two," we're quick to shout.
    "What's that?" And he cups his ear like he
can't hear us. "Say what?" he asks again.
"Three, including Mama? No, no, four?
Including brother and sister who still at
home? No, not that either, members, it's
just the two of you. And God, and let him
be the sounding board, let him be the sole
advisor. You tell Janie and Paul a secret
about your woman and you go home and

43

lay your head on your pillow and you sleep it away like a bad dream, but Janie still thinking about it, and every time your woman walking by, Paul envisioning your private pain and he breathing in it its own spark of life. No, member. Noooo," and he allows that word to linger so it escapes halfway between a sigh and a moan. "Nooo. And who can find a virtuous woman? For her price is far above rubies. And virtue's not something you can buy, is it? You either have it through the spirit of the Lord being implanted in you from birth or you spend your whole life searching. And Major," he turns to my son wiping the sweat from his forehead, "Major, I think you got it, I think you might be one of the lucky souls on this Earth who found it." He is nearly singing now, and he lifts his feet one by one into the air and pumps in slow heavy motion down the steps until he reaches the couple. "I think you got it, and when you got it, best to hold on to it with all your miiight." And that last sentiment is so nearly a song that an ordinarily quiet woman who sang soprano in the choir with me starts clapping her hands and stomping her feet, shouting, "Yes," slow at first, then faster and faster still. The preacher mingles his own words with her shouts, then he nods at the organist, and with everyone joining, even the children, belts out:

Let Jesus lead you
Let Jesus lead you
Let Jesus lead you
All the way
All the way from
Earth to Heaven
Let Jesus lead you, all the way

I stand too. I can hear my own voice, heavy but sweet, shining above the rest, and I'm keeping time with my feet, balancing on each alternately, and swinging my body when I can manage, singing all the while. Members behind me raise their rattles and tambourines and clamor down the aisle.

He's a mighty good leader
He's a mighty good leader
He's a mighty good leader
All the way
All the way from
Earth to Heaven
Let Jesus lead you all the way

And some are down on their knees between the pews, their heads swaying to the front, then back again, and others are stomping in a circle around the pulpit, their

45

words spewing out in tongues amid the chorus.

Let Him lead you
Let Him lead you
Let Him lead you
Let Him lead you
Let Him lead you
All down the highway
Let Him lead you
Just like He lead my mother
Lead my father
Let Him lead you
Let Him lead you

We all quiet down after a spell. Even before the dancing, it was hotter inside the church than outside it, and we sit and we fan the sweat glistening on our brows. I lift the cloth of my dress off my sticky skin. The preacher leans into Major and clears his throat. He asks him to make a vow to love Eliza until death does them part. The few times there was a wedding at neighboring plantations, the preacher would make the bride and groom promise devotion until distance, or white folks, intervened; it was different in other ways too. The groom wore patched pants, and sometimes Kentucky jeans. Major, though, is wearing his daddy's old suit. With the white gloves and tall beaver, he could pass for my late husband. Same burnt orange skin, same tight red curls, same coal-black eyes, and I have to look away.

Now it is time to jump the broom, backward while the preacher holds it a foot off the floor. Eliza scales it, but Major's foot hitches, and we all know what that means. The crowd laughs: "She's the boss, now." "Better lend her those pants now, boy." Hearing those sentiments, as I walk back down the aisle, I try not to wince.

I can smell the food from the lip of the church, the sizzling fried pork and creamy custard pies, the greens, potato salad and yams, the spices I added to the meat and rice for boudin. I walk over to the grandest table and not too long after I sit, Jericho carries me a plate. I take a bite. Generally, I am hard on myself; my food in particular never seems to come out as good as my mama's, but today it seems like she was leaning over my back shaking the salt for me, and instead of the Lord, I silently thank her. People approach as I eat. Sharecroppers from my own field; grown men and women I delivered and set in their new mothers' arms; teachers who'd taught Major, and some work with Eliza now; Link, who reunited former slaves after the war. For the longest time, I'd push her to find my mama, and she traveled all over the state of Louisiana, in churches and white folk agencies too, but to no avail.

She sits down with her plate touching mine. She is wearing a simple skirt and blouse, a bucket hat. I compliment her on it all. She has a strong gap between her teeth; she is as long as I am wide, but our skin is the same dark brown, and when our arms touch, they could be of the same body. The sun is setting, and the heat is thin enough for wind to pass through. People have pulled out banjos, fiddles and drums for dancing, the Buzzard Lope and the Cakewalk. Link and I watch them for a long time, not needing to say a word to read each other's thoughts.

"I had a dream about Henry last night."

"Oh?" I look up. It is like the sweetness of the day brought out Link's secret pain.

"He was standing right beside me; we were sipping lemonade on my own porch. But my heart was heavy. I don't think he's coming back."

I shake my head, no. What is there to say? "Whether he does or not it's best to assume the worst, be ready for that outcome," I say.

She nods. She understands, but it is her son.

"You think Eliza's mama cared for that carrying-on from the preacher?" Link asks.

I can tell she's trying to get her mind in a good place, to allow herself to enjoy this day.

"I could see her people in the front row," she goes on, "holding their mouths like they were drinking lemonade that wasn't cut with enough sugar."

"Whether they abide it or not, no way I would close a marriage ceremony without it."

"I know that, but do they? People like that more into silent prayer."

"Silent what?"

And Link lifts her shoulders and shifts her chest out and starts moving her lips but no sound comes out, and we are steady laughing. Eliza's people walk by and I shut up on the spot, straighten up my face. It is no use though. They seem to sense they interrupted something.

"Was an awful nice ceremony," I say with a smile.

"Very nice, exceeded my expectations," the mother, Cyrile, says, her face still scrunched up like her breakfast didn't agree with her. "And the food, we have to get going but I can smell you really know your way around a kitchen." She must mean it as a compliment, but the way her mouth is set, she could be saying, *Sister, you know you stewed those beans in an outhouse.*

"You sure are missing out, Mama." Louis is halfway through his plate, even standing up. There is a speck of barbecue sauce right under his chin, and I have an urge to wipe it off same way I'd do Major, but I hold my hand back. Anyway his mama does it for me.

"Well, we ought to be going now," she snaps at him when he's done, and he gulps a cup of sweet lemonade. His hair is slick and soft and he leans over and kisses my cheek, rubbing his belly as he walks away.

"She leaving miiighty early," Link says.

"They do got to get all the way back north."

"Still, her daughter's wedding. I'd be the last one standing."

"I don't pretend to understand the ways of those people."

I take another sip of tea; everybody else is having more than that, strawberry water with cane sugar and whiskey, and you'll see the effects come an hour. The quietest men will swoop taken women off their feet; the softest women will raise their voices in their

50

sisters' faces, and I wonder all of a sudden about Jericho; he is with the children dancing to old Sally Walker, almost indistinct from the others, but I can see his eyes. Behind them, he is elsewhere.

My own child and his new wife are greeting people, making their rounds.

"They make quite the pair," Link says.

"Who?" I ask.

"Who you think? The bride and groom. And she couldn't look any prettier."

"No, I suppose not."

"Happy too. That's the thing. Sometimes you see these people jump the broom and they can barely look each other in the eye. They just doing it cause they got a child need minding or mama who thinks it's time to take up the family way. But not them. Seem like this was an idea all their own."

"All their own indeed," I say, and we laugh the way people laugh when either one of them could have spoken, their minds are so connected. It is a hearty laugh, from deep down somewhere, but it is light too because she knew the joke already.

They do look happy. It is hard to watch them period, but especially without Isaiah beside me. Most days I can pretend he is out on the farm; he spent most of his waking hours there and I didn't begrudge him

51

that. Those early years were the cotton ones. Working on the halves, Isaiah would fill a sack with fiber he pulled from the dried bolls, then carry the sack to the wagon, weigh it, dump it out clean, and some days he'd report picking over five hundred pounds. It didn't matter though, not when it was time to settle up, and Mr. Dennis's mouth would run in circles about the cost of seeds, tools, jackets, fertilizer; my husband couldn't write enough to record, and even if he could, no white man would have read it; more times than not, we'd come out with fifty cents for the month. "This little bitty money," he'd toss it at the table, but I'd stretch it, baby. I'd sell eggs and mend seams, and he'd fix clocks and guns, and we'd stretch it, and inside our house, we didn't talk about Mr. Dennis. We didn't think about him either. Because of that it is the nights that are merciless, the nights and occasions like these —

"You any keener on her?" Link asks.

I look at Link. We came here together after the war. Different plantations, but both motherless, we'd walk the turn row to town together. People say I have started to favor her, or her me, not just in the way we laugh with our heads back and our shoulders shaking, or because we say in our scratched-up voices *all right* instead of *hello* when someone greets us. No, our noses have plumped, our eyes have narrowed, the skin on our necks is slack, and more than once I've had to inform a young person we weren't born sisters. I say that to say it is not possible to lie to her.

I shake my head.

"Time has a way of working that stuff out. And babies."

"Lord willing," I say. Though a part of me is afraid of their new family, on behalf of Jericho, sure, but also for me. I hadn't foreseen living so long. Most people I talk to are half my age; Link got the sugar and lost three toes on her left foot, my son and his bride haven't made it to my table yet, and though the pig was masterful, I have a taste in the back of my tongue like soot. When they finally reach me, it feels like the only way to purge that metallic flavor is to speak.

Before I can even say *Congratulations,* I start.

"Eliza, can I take you aside for a moment?"

She follows me to a part of the yard where the music isn't swallowing our words whole.

"It was a beautiful ceremony," she says. "And the food, I haven't tried it, but everybody is complimenting us. I told them it was all —"

"Jericho James has just as much a right to Major as you do," I cut in. "He's his son."

"I know that," she talks in that squeak she uses and for the first time I want to lay her across my knee the way I would my own daughters. They aren't with me — one followed her husband north and the other one followed hope in the same direction, but I'd take my own hand to them both if they hadn't learned by now that there are times when it's safe to let your voice ring out in this world.

My words are stuck in my throat. I didn't expect her to mold to my touch.

"Well, if you know that, then you know he's gotta start sleeping there like it's his home. It was improper at first; boy needed a mama after his own run off, and I had to see to his meals, teach him how to use the bathroom, clean after himself, but now he's older and I'm not going to be here forever."

"I know that."

"Oh. You know that, huh? Well, see to it that he sleeps with you beginning tonight then. First night will set the tone for the rest of your marriage. He'll think of you a certain way if you let him know at the jump he's one of you."

"He is. Me letting him know that won't be an act or a show, just the truth. Listen, Miss Josephine, I made a vow up there in front of that preacher and all of you to wed myself with Major, and I didn't just mean Major, I meant Jericho James, and you."

"Well, good then." I nod. It wasn't too often I caught myself speechless. I credit it to the fact that the girl knows her letters, not makeshift from the slave master's daughter who wasn't but nine years old herself, but from an actual teacher, who had been trained by a white woman. I was proud of that when Major first told me, but the more time went on it began to unsteady me. I had thought of the world a certain way, but a different picture of it had been painted and there were countries I hadn't even known existed.

"All right then," I repeat. "It was a mighty fine ceremony." And I walk off adjusting my hat. I slip on the way back to my seat and more than a few young men reach for my arm, but I steady myself; even if they hadn't been there, I would have been all right.

On our way home, we glimpse the new white neighbors out front. They don't live but a rock's throw from me, the only property in my line of sight that I don't own.

The small farm used to be the overseer's, and I can't glance at it without wanting to spit. Now these new people grow a few crops: corn, and I've noticed them picking peas and bedding sweet potatoes. They moved in a few months back, just finished closing in their chickens with hog wire, but I haven't ventured to say five words to them. Today, despite my misgivings, I feel like nothing can touch me.

"All right," I nod, and tip my hat. A young couple, no kids yet. The man has always been the one to speak; I catch him some mornings selling fish from an ice chest. The girl just drags behind him like a dog enduring a bad foot. As we talk, guests from the wedding ride by on the winding gravel. Oaks flank the lane, which is just wide enough for one mule at a time. I know the full names of everybody who passes. They wave at me, then shoot one quick glance at the neighbors and speed off.

"We didn't want to interrupt. We heard the noise out front. Sounds like you had a party." This from the man of course.

"My son got married."

"Married, huh? Well, congratulations. Who's the lucky girl?"

I nod behind me though I know they can't see that far back. "Gal in the white."

"Well, I'll be. We didn't formally meet, but my name is Vern; this is my wife, Charlotte."

"How do you do?"

They reach their hands out, but I know better than to take them. Most of their kind live closer to town and for that very reason, we try to stay put. Link's nephew is the one to stuff mattresses and weave baskets; Isaiah's cousins sell charcoal and animal traps; we run our own syrup mills, break our own horses, carve our own tables, cut our own hair, and aside from selling cotton or trading in the store, our paths and white people's do not converge.

"Well, it's been a long day," I say. "I'll be heading back in."

"Of course, of course. We'll be seeing you around then. Say, my wife could use some company during the day. I notice you're home —"

I turn back to him. I would have been more surprised if Jesus had turned up at the front door and asked me for a cup of sugar. Not but one hundred feet apart in residence but this white man has his well and I have mine. Yes, our clotheslines only hang a few feet apart, but as soon as my items dry, I fold them into my drawer. It's the white folks whose underthings swing in the night breeze.

"Listen, I got children and grandchildren who need me. Clients too." I don't deliver as many babies as I had in my youth, but some mothers still call. "I cook three meals and take in some laundry." I raise my hands. I'm more than a little surprised at how my words have streamed out like they'd been waiting for him. "I'm still wondering when the Lord is going to add more hours to the day, but until he hears me . . ." I trail off. They laugh at the joke about God, and I close the door and click the bolt behind me.

I don't normally lock up. In fact you can find me rocking on my porch most nights until the wind cuts through my shawl. The Klan isn't deep here like they used to be in Link's sister's side of town. Not only that, I'm still marveling at the change: down the hill, the houses were so close to the marsh mosquitos ate us for breakfast, lunch, dinner, and dessert; either that, or we closed the windows and suffocated in the heat. Here the night air feels like God close up, whispering his secrets, and I'm liable to stare at the butter beans and mustard greens my husband laid the groundwork for like it's the seventh day.

Today is different though. Aside from the

wedding, which was of course a joyous occasion, it seems like those neighbors got something sticky about themselves they were trying to pass off, press inside me, and I need more of a barrier than normal. I collapse on my bed before I even take off my shoes. I don't know how long I am out, but when I hear the knock it's clear it's been sounding for some time. I jerk up, reach for my kerosene lamp and light it. Like I said, there isn't any Klan, not yet, but Link talked about them like they were supernatural, an army of ghosts riding around with bullets peppered through them. Not only that, there was burning and looting, lynching too. Link's kin had to stay by me for two weeks last winter after those devils shot a man for standing in front of a white woman at the general store. The memory of it sits low in my mind today, and for that reason I look through the hole my son drilled through the door before I answer. Oh. It is only Jericho.

I open up fast, set a pot of milk on the wood stove to boil; there are always roasted peanuts and he grabs a handful and tosses them back.

He sits down at the table. I had heard Eliza tell Link that today was the best day of her life. She would never forget it, but Jericho looks like he won't forget it either, only for opposite reasons.

"What is it? You look like somebody been hainted." The fireplace is out but I reignite it, add a couple pieces of lumber to the pit.

He shakes his head but he doesn't say a word.

"What is it? I thought you was sleeping over by them tonight."

He shakes his head again.

I stand all of a sudden, and the pine floor seems to bend with my weight. The sadness is too much for me to bear. I only met his mama a few times, but I'd been shocked when she up and left a three-month-old in my arms. A baby who had gotten used to the breast, and I had to drip milk from my cows onto his tongue with a medicine dropper. I shudder each time I remember the nights: he'd rumble awake at the sound of my breath shifting and it would start up again, that interminable wail that I'd take to my grave. My life had not been easy by any account, and I was surprised to realize, old as I was, finished as I thought I was, that that wail would be the hardest thing I'd endure.

I reach for my coat. "Where is she? I told her it was your house. I told her if she couldn't abide that, we wouldn't abide her. In so many words, I told her that." I can hear myself huffing. I have always been a little too quick to anger; anybody who knows me knows you never have to wonder what I am thinking, but that trait looks different on me now. I don't have to see a reflection to know it can read as sad. I can't always keep my footing these days.

"She told me I could stay there, Mama," he says, reaching for my hand.

It takes a while for his words to hold; I had become so worked up.

"What do you mean?" I ask. "Then why are you here?"

"I wanted to be here, Mama. I didn't want to be anywhere else."

"Oh," I sit down. The milk is bubbling, but I'd get it in a second. "Oh," I repeat. "Well, I suppose that's okay," I say. Him staying is more than okay. "I got some pig lips I set aside for us this morning," I say.

He nods. "I didn't have much of an appetite earlier."

"That's understandable."

Though he is twelve we still sleep in the same room, and when I am done with the dishes, I lie down on the bed opposite him. I close my eyes, a drift away from that other world, unrecognizable faces and names already pulsing inside my mind, when he

61

pats my arm.

"Mama?"

"Yes, son?"

"Can you tell me the story again?"

"It's too late," I say. I don't remember what I just gave up but it was sweet, I know that, as sweet as anything I can dredge up from my own, real life.

"Please," he whispers.

I prop up on one arm. Maybe I spoil him.

"He's a black man in this world," Major has scolded me. "You got him used to sweetness when life gon' be tart."

"Somebody's got to do it," I always shout back. "Doesn't make it any more tart because you have known sweetness. If anything, the sweetness levels it out for you." That's what I'd say, but I have no way of knowing.

Of course Major isn't only protecting Jericho. He resents me. I didn't tell my own children stories, didn't have the time to, and if I had the time, I certainly didn't have the breath. I was still a child crafting jump ropes from vines when I was ripped off that plantation, and it took me past adulthood to see straight again, to be inside my body when I was hauling the plow, hammering nails on the fences, planting the cotton, cutting the onions, thickening the roux, marching through the streets with the stink from white people's dirty clothes wafting off my head, balancing water from the wells, washing and boiling the clothes. I used lye to make soap and wheat bran for starch. I'd hang skirts and short pants on plum bushes. Then I'd heat the iron on the stove, cover it with beeswax, clear it, wet the garments, and run that iron back and forth. At least once a month, a bell would ring for me and I'd carry my sassafras and castor oil to a screaming woman's house to thin the time between her contractions. I soaked beans and braided hair and sewed dresses for my children, but I didn't bother to tell them I loved them.

"Okay," I say now. "What story should it be?"

"The one where you died and came back to life."

I nod. That is his favorite, and as far as memories go, it is harmless.

"You not sick of that one?" I ask, buying time.

He shakes his head.

"All right then."

I clear my throat and lean my head against the pillow. It is hard looking back. As close as I have to be to dying it is easier to look forward than to look back.

JOSEPHINE

My mama had two babies before me. A sister and a brother too, but I never met them. Mama said they had more sense than I did, that they only needed to smell the world to know there was nothing inside it for them. So she was relieved when I came out, when I breathed. She didn't get close to me anyway, assuming I would catch on too, that I'd be gone any minute, but I stuck around. I held my head up, I sat, I stood, I fed myself cut-up swamp rabbits or fish, I spoke. I ran. And she wiped my mouth and hemmed my skirts; she taught me how to make beds out of dry grass and talk to white folks with my head down and my words dull. But she held on to her heart too; she didn't let it lead her.

Then one morning she was boiling clothes outside the cabins, and Vera screamed for her to come quick. My mama dropped a wet shirt on her foot and didn't flinch at the burn. She raced up to the cabin where Vera nursed all the babies too young to hold their heads up. Mama realized then that she was wrong — all the hope she thought she had buried with the other children had been there all along, snaking its way through her. She reached me, and it was too late, I was gone.

Vera closed my eyes, clutched my mama to her, and let her wail.

Still there was no use. Vera alerted Tom and Missus, and they told my daddy to carve a pine box, and Mama said the worst part was that she had let herself be fooled again.

They let her hold the body one night. She had to burn sage to keep the gnats and wasps off me, and she did the only thing she could do: she slept beside me on a pallet on the dirt floor. She was awakened sometime before dusk. She stood, but she said it wasn't her feet she stood on. They were heavier with calluses and age, the feet of a woman who had worked in fields. She said too that she carried a weight on her she wasn't accustomed to, and even climbing off her pallet was strenuous. The biggest change was in her mind: it had emptied out and narrowed in a way that relieved her.

She knew to make haste for the swamplands. *Don't let the sun rise before you're back,* her mother's voice sounded in her own mind, the same way she had taught her to stitch moccasins, or cut the watermelon for its rind to rinse her face. That voice was gentle but firm, not like hers, which was heavy as a man's people said, and she knew.

She reached back just as the night sky was fading. She said a pigeon followed her all the way home. She didn't have to run. She carried a skirt full of green berries, and she built a fire to boil a tea. I still wasn't breathing, but she tilted my head and watched the liquid stream down my chin. *Call those things which be not as though they were.* She could hear her mama's voice but it was her own trembling fingers that lifted the kettle, tilted the cup. It wasn't until Vera walked in that I sat up and asked for water. They didn't give me too much; they were nervous at first, but after I finished drinking, I wanted grits and they boiled them over the fireplace, ladled them with fatback, and let me eat bowl after bowl.

After that, Vera gave me the biggest piece of ham at dinner. I stayed out the fields and just played with Miss Sally all day long; she was the one taught me to read. I started seeing that woman then too, that long brown trail of a woman. She was from another world, but she felt like me; I mean, when she spoke, it felt like the words came out my own mind. Most important though, I got to sit with the Revisioners, sing with them, pray with them. Foresee with them.

AVA

2017

The next day, I run some last-minute errands, go back to the block for that old photograph of Mama Josephine, alert the power company, pay the balance on my storage, and then there is something that I've been putting off long enough. I need to see my mother. I'm always nervous to make that ride, and today is no different. I've never lived farther than twenty minutes away from her, but I still don't visit more than once a quarter. Even then it's out of obligation, not desire. I've been slow to get on my feet. Married the wrong man, majored in the wrong subject. I have a chemistry degree but can't translate that into a job paying more than $40k, and that seemed like a lot when I was in my twenties and still married, but every time I looked up, there was another girl texting Byron, simple girls who spelled love *luv,* who sent half-naked pictures of themselves, their titties sky-high. I worked up the courage to put him out, I loved myself enough to risk it, but not three months after he was gone, I'd drained my savings flat. And that's all right, I guess. I stopped ordering takeout from Martin's Wine Cellar, started working weekends at Vincent's. There was a balance scale set up in Mr. Jeff's office, but he filled only the left side of it, so it drooped. I used to think that was how my life was, that the filled section was the reality and the empty one was my dreams, and I just had to come to terms with it. But whenever I'm about to see my mother, my self-acceptance begins to wobble.

I pull onto her block. She rented an apartment uptown after Katrina, then once she'd gutted all the walls, and replaced the roof on her old house in the Tremé, she insisted on going back. "Home," she'd said. "Nothing like it," though her block is all white now, mostly transplants. There's still Miss Brown and Mr. Davilier on either side of her, but every other house is a short-term rental, and even Miss Brown is considering selling to developers.

I hear gospel music from the inside.

Give me You, everything else can wait

69

She doesn't lock her door anymore, and instead of knocking, I open up. She is finishing one of her sessions. She'd owned her law firm for twenty years, ran it out of the Poydras Center, and she did well on divorces and slip-and-falls primarily, but when I went off to college, she closed up shop, decided to take classes to become a doula. That was around the time she stopped putting ham hocks and sausages in her red beans, started meditating each morning. I wasn't surprised. My whole childhood, people would come from all over the city for her counsel. One day I leafed through the top drawer of her dresser and found, amid old obituaries and worn stones, scraps of paper asking for me to get the part in the play, for the client to win full custody. All those things had happened, and I was just then seeing her fingerprints.

She said working with the girls had changed her life, and I see the changes sometimes. She's slower to anger, I confide in her more, matters I'd normally keep to myself, like how I felt when my divorce papers went through. Now her clients, about seven girls, circle around her with their eyes closed, their palms faceup on their thighs. My mother doesn't look at me, just nods in the direction of the living room, and I know enough to remember what that means: sit down and shut up, and I oblige.

The girls start chanting as I sit, incoherent sounds but the blend of them together is like tasting my mama's potato salad, the old version with the real mayonnaise. I close my eyes too. As much as it unnerves me to see her now, I miss this part, how sturdy she could be, how sturdy I was on account of growing up beside her. She would walk me to school every morning and tell me things with her hand in mine: three squeezes, for instance, stood for *I love you.* She taught me to visualize a white light encasing me, protecting me from harm. "Nobody evil can get through that light," she'd say. "Nobody," she'd repeat. And people tried. The kids always had a bone to pick with my color; my daddy didn't come around but once every blue moon, but I got by all that. It didn't break me, because there was at least a small chance that that white light she mentioned was blooming from inside me.

"Just breathe," she says to the girls now. "Just breathe. Whatever comes up through the breath is okay. We don't have to turn our back on it, we don't have to look away. No, sit with it, welcome it in, ask it what it has to say. Remember, Yemaya, the Virgin

Mary, and your own divine mother sit right above you. They're always there: they're threaded in your heart, they're woven in your words, they move through you, there is nowhere you can be where they are not steady, holding your hand."

My mother stands up and walks the room, cutting between women whose bellies sit on their legs. One woman with yellow hair threaded through her braids is sobbing. My mother leans down and squeezes her shoulder.

"Ask her to take it, beg her to relieve you of it. You can't get rid of it without her; ask her to weed out all the jealousy, the pain, the heartache." She looks around. "Somebody in here got some grief as big as this room; ask her to dig it out of you right now, and she'll do it. Ask her to lift it off your chest. You don't need it anymore." She shifts to a whisper. "Feel her release it from you, she loves it, you don't have to be embarrassed to hand it off, it's her joy to receive it, see her cradle it, see her rock it in her love, and watch it turn golden. Watch it turn golden," she repeats. She stands there for a while in silence, then she walks back to the front of the room and sits again. She just turned fifty-eight, but she seems lovelier each year. She doesn't do makeup, doesn't need to. Her waist-length dredlocks are wrapped in a bright blue-and-pink patterned scarf, and she wears a long cotton black dress that hugs her soft curves when it sways. She has cancer though. Has for three years, and won't get chemo for it.

She calls it poison, and she takes her herbs and seems to live at the acupuncture clinic on Canal. I don't worry about her in a way that shows, but in the back of my mind I'm always primed for the phone to ring.

She releases the girls in a prayer, and they approach her one by one to say goodbye.

"Love you, Gladys," they whisper in her ear as they embrace.

They are teenage girls, many with two jobs, none with stable housing; they've got baby daddies and bills holding them below water, like me, but my mother has lifted them to another state just now, and it's miraculous to behold.

When it's just us, she walks over and tries to hug me, and I allow it for a minute but not much longer.

I know she's not going to be happy with me, moving in with the other side, so I want to lay it out fast.

"Mama," I say, but she cuts me off.

"Girl with the yellow braids lost her baby last time. She needs a lot of support. A lot of support." She looks up at me like she's coming out of a trance. "Anyway, I knew you were coming over today. I dreamed that I was on an airplane and we turned back before it ascended fully. Knew immediately what it meant."

"Mama, what does an airplane have to do with me?"

"Expect the unexpected, it said. My grandmother, Lucille, she talks to me through transportation. Anyway, you look good, glowing. You off from work?"

"More or less," I say.

"Uh oh. More or less, come into the kitchen. I'm going to need my tea for 'more or less.' Expect the unexpected," she repeats as we walk.

Her kitchen was updated years ago but it still seems new with her granite island countertop overlooking the living room and the beige-and-coffee-brown tiled backsplash. Her floors are hardwood but there are Persian rugs that pop with color, piercing blues and orange and African masks on the wall from a trip to Zimbabwe two winters ago. She framed her favorite inspirational phrases, *God is all there is. He is in me and he is me.* There's a pot of jambalaya on the stove. No sausage or shrimp inside, of course, but you wouldn't know it from the smell, and I might as well be ten years old again wondering if I can have a scoop of ice cream after dinner for dessert.

"Mama, I moved," I say.

She places a kettle of water on to boil and then walks over to stand beside me.

I know what she's thinking, *Again,* and I wait for her to say it but it doesn't come.

"It must be nice," she says smiling. "You look happy, it must be nice." She sounds almost desperate to believe what she's saying.

"It is, Mama. I want you to see it. It's really nice."

"Well, where is it?" she asks. I hear the kettle go off. But she doesn't get up to pour the water. She just looks at me.

"I moved in with Grandma Martha," I say, and she takes it in. I remember when King was a baby and I would tell him no. He wouldn't always react right away; sometimes he had to find his way over to the scream.

I keep talking to fill the void.

"She needed extra help at night. I was just laid off, and even when I was working, I was missing King. Some of the kids at school were after him. I told you about the fight."

She nods.

"She's paying me my old salary. Double

when you consider it's rent-free. Can you imagine what I can do with that money? No rent to pay. By the end of the year, I was thinking I could have enough saved up to buy." I lower my voice. I'm scared just saying it. "A townhouse or something, nothing too big, but . . ."

She smiles, and I feel the release of the weight of the words inside me.

"What do you think?" I ask. "I would have asked you first, but it just came to me, like inspiration, you always say, and I didn't want to have to ask for permission. I'm thirty-four now. I'm a grown-ass woman, and I guess I just got tired of running everything by my mama first." I want to keep talking to smooth over the awkwardness building, but there's nothing more to say.

She doesn't respond for a while, just keeps staring at me.

"You did the right thing," she says finally. "It seems to me you did the right thing." She nods, while she thinks it over, like somebody tasting food, considering if she should add salt. "I mean, I always thought you would be such a good doula. If you wanted to try that now, it seems like it'd be the perfect time. You just have a special way with people when they're not at their best.

When you were a little girl, you'd always know when I needed an extra hug. On airplanes, grown people would sit next to you, tell you their secrets, stories they'd never shared with anyone else." She stops herself. "Never mind, you did right, girl. I'm proud of you," and she is that warm and loving woman I've glimpsed more with her clients than with me, but I'll take it, especially because I never have to wonder what my mother is thinking. If she says it, it's real.

"Thank you, Mama," I say.

She goes for the tea.

"King in school," she goes on. "You all closer with each other." She is still nodding as she passes me my cup. "That all sounds right on, baby girl," she repeats.

"Thank you, Mama," I say. "I'm so relieved to hear you say that."

She pauses to drink. "I'm not going to be here forever, you know."

I set my own cup down. I hate it when she talks like this.

"It's true, it's true. Might as well face it, it's the one thing we can count on. And you need to be self-sufficient once I'm gone, like you're doing," she adds. "Like you're doing."

I see her skin has become looser around

the neck. I've heard enough this week about mortality, so when she suggests going to the back to work in her garden, I am right behind her.

She is nimble and quick on her feet. There's a chair planted in the dirt and I sit and watch her while she knifes the stems of okra just above their caps. She talks while she works: she says that she still remembers the smell of the earth on her grandmother Lucille's farm, that she never met her great-great-grandmother but that she knew she was a slave, that she's been thinking about her more and more lately.

"Josephine," she says, like I've never heard her say the name before. "Isn't that pretty? I almost named you after her, but your daddy —" she shakes her head.

I tell her how happy I've been since I've moved, like all my mistakes from the past have been upended. I tell her about dinner the night before, how well I slept.

I lose time sitting there and when I look at my watch, it is after three, and I have to pick up King.

"Kiss him for me, you hear?" she calls out, running her fingers through the vegetables in her pail, and then she starts to say something, stops herself, then starts up again.

"And that lady, I know she's good to you now," she says. "And I'm happy for you, I am. But don't forget you work for her. Don't forget what she's capable of. You're her granddaughter, so it's different, but I have to tell you, she wasn't good to me. It was a different time back then, but I never forgot it."

There she is, my old mother, but I don't get upset hearing that. It soothes me rather; in this time of change, it is nice to be put at ease.

"Don't get so caught up in the surroundings. Remember who you are. What did I used to tell you? Brilliant, beautiful girl. You have the power of your ancestors coursing through your veins."

And I could have and I did. Until I met King's daddy and twelve months later, I had dropped out of school and was cleaning up honey mustard sauce at the Burger King on Bullard. I went back to college when King turned two, finished even, but by then, the kids who had attended Ben Franklin with me had lapped me. I head west on I-10 now, get off on Claiborne, make a left on Napoleon, hit St. Charles. The Tulane girls run up and down the trolley tracks with their itty-bitty shorts on, and with the soft rhythm of the streetcars growing fainter in my ear,

the mansions' gas lamps flickering, I pass
them by.

Things are smooth for the next few weeks. I am tentative at first, a new guest, asking where the dry towels are in the morning, tiptoeing around Binh to pour the rum for the Dr. No's my boy at Cure taught me, but by the end of the week I have made myself at home. I am calling up to King about cinnamon rolls, reorganizing the pantry so my grits are in the forefront. King is rifling through the fridge on his own initiative to make double meat sandwiches and lying down on the sofa to play *Fortnite.* Of course he makes friends, but it's different this time. They're little girls mostly, skinny white ones with blond hair they pull back in scrunchies, which are in again I guess. The main ones are named Harper and Claire, they wear tight yoga pants and neon shirts, and they wait with him until I pull up; then they follow him to the car, passing him notes, and hugging him, all,

"Love ya, King."

And to my absolute shock and horror, he responds. "Love you too."

"Love you?" I turn to the backseat as we pull out. "What the hell is that about?"

He laughs. "Mama, they don't really love me, it's just how they say *see you soon.*"

"They better damn well say *see you soon* then," I say. "I don't like that," I add.

"Calm down, Mama, they're nice," he goes on. "You said you wanted me to get comfortable."

"I didn't mean that comfortable," I mumble, but I hear him. It's nice to know he's relaxing. In our old house, he'd bus home alone, and scramble together fragments of leftovers from the fridge. Here, I heat up exotic meals from the night before and sit with him while he starts his homework. It's strange at first. I'm always trying to vacuum or chop onions only for Grandma to remind me there's somebody here to do that for me, but I start to settle into the quiet. I hadn't known how tired I was until I had the chance to sit down.

On the other hand, every now and then I yearn for a space of my own. Nothing outright unpleasant has happened. But as big as the house is, sharing it with Grandma makes it seem like close quarters. I am privy to the sounds of her sneezing, her clearing her throat, her women's group filling up the dining room table knitting personalized pussy hats and weeping about Trump. She takes a nap at noon sprawled out on the sofa and her mouth hangs open. She usually dresses like her old self, but sometimes she comes downstairs uncharacteristically, once without her teeth and then a different time wearing large gold rings I wouldn't have known she owned strewn out on every finger. I haven't smelled the foul smell since that first time, but I am always on the lookout for it, and as much as I love her, I didn't grow up with her, not really, and the intimacy of her decline feels too up-front.

It's not only that, I can't sleep, and when I do sleep, I don't stay that way. I wake up and stare at the window. I've been having the same kinds of dreams as the first night, ghastly dreams that light up a sickening feeling I can't place, and I am up with a start but it's hard to remember anything concrete, only that someone was chasing me and nearly at my heels.

It doesn't matter. I don't dare complain. My money is piling up in my top drawer, cash because Grandma says she won't allow me to throw half away to the man. I don't fight her on it, but I count the bills each night for comfort. And King is happy. Every day he shares something he's learned: coding, playwriting, film editing. For a midsemester project, he and the girls put together a music video to "24K Magic." The camera shook so much it made me dizzy, and the girls danced like, well, bless their hearts, it was sweet to watch. I was just glad to see King's curiosity is being stoked, and he's safe — that's all that matters.

The little white girls he befriends have mothers. One day I'm waiting outside my car for King and I see them hurrying over to me, turning to each other and whispering, then picking up their pace. I'm on guard because of how pressed they seem but if I read it right, they are also giddy. They both have blond highlights, their brown roots poking out to say hello, but one wears lipstick and high boots with leggings and one is in workout gear with her hair pulled back in a bun.

"Are you King's mom?" the overdressed one asks. She's already smiling like she just can't help herself.

I nod.

"I'm Claire's mom." She holds her hand out.

"And I'm Harper's," the other one follows suit.

I wait for the problem, for them to say something crazy about King hanging out with their girls. I prepare my response. If I'm honest, it's been there waiting. I'll tell them that King has a charm, that people from all walks of life are attracted to him, that it's always been that way. I'll tell them it's their girls who call him every night and who initiate the texts, I've checked the phone. I'll tell them that it's harmless, that all they're texting about is Bruno Mars, the Weeknd, and Janelle Monae, and he teaches them slang from his old school, but he doesn't use curse words, I make sure of that myself. If they want it to stop, I'll tell them to tell their girls to leave him alone, that King has options. But they are still smiling.

"We think it's so great that the girls have taken to him so," the dressy one says.

"Oh?"

"Yeah, I mean they've always had each other. We went to Loyola together and the girls were in a nanny share, but it's so nice to see them branching out." This is from the athlete.

"I can already tell Claire's more confident," the dressy one says. "The teacher says she's raising her hand more in class. She used to be so painfully shy, except with Harper." The woman seems to be tearing up.

"We even have a name for them."

"Three's Company," the athlete says.

"Three's Company," the dressy one repeats.

"I know it's cheesy," the athlete concedes, "but we think it's so cute."

"Did you ever watch that show?" the dressy one asks. "You're probably too young. You look way younger than we do. We started late."

"And I had to get IVF," the athlete interjects.

The dressy one starts humming the theme song to the show, and the athlete joins her.

Sure enough, Three's Company walk out now, arms linked, King in the middle. The mothers are singing, filling in the chorus with dance moves not unlike their daughters' in the video. And a tension I didn't know I was carrying seems to clear.

I'm so relieved I could join them in singing.

Instead we wave goodbye and get into the car. Grandma was napping when I left so King and I drive to Audubon Park for him to skateboard, then to my favorite snowball stand for a medium blue coconut cup for me and a large strawberry cheesecake for him. We walk down Magazine Street, window-shop in antique stores I can't afford, and that used to bother me, but it feels like there's a change on the horizon and I look in at the French side tables and armoires with an interest that feels justified, like it might lead me somewhere. The whole while I'm walking, I can't get that song out of my head. I was too young to watch the show when it aired but Grandma Martha would play the reruns in the summer.

Come and dance on our floor
Take a step that is new
We've a lovable space that needs your
　　face
Three's company too

It's dinnertime when I get back. King changes his clothes, and I look for Grandma Martha. She's not downstairs or in her room. I check the library with its wall-to-wall bookshelves, Jane Austen, Ernest Hemingway, and a first-edition copy of *To Kill A Mockingbird* that Grandma Martha says she rereads each year. She's not there either, and not in the study, the garage, or even out back in the yard with the fountain. Finally, I remember the laundry room and wind my way past the old servants' quarters, and there she is, sitting in front of the washing machine hunched down, rubbing the crook in her neck. She's wearing a bold pink sweater and red slacks. It would be unusual for her to choose just one of those colors, but her having paired them is alarming.

"Grandma Martha," I say, approaching. "Is everything okay?"

"I've been looking everywhere for you, girl," she snaps, and there is rage in her eyes.

She's never spoken to me like that, but I am troubled more than offended.

"Are you okay?" I repeat.

"No." She bursts into tears. "I can barely move my neck," she says, "and you were supposed to be here."

I settle in next to her when she won't budge. I hold out my arms and she falls into them. Her face is wet against my chest. I look down and see a small line of blood trickling down her temple.

"Grandma, what happened?" I repeat, louder this time, reaching for a Kleenex in my purse. She says it's nothing, that she didn't notice her bathroom medicine cabinet was open, and I can see the flow of the blood has already ebbed. As she's explaining, her medical alert goes off.

"Nine-one-one, what's your emergency?"

She tells them it was a mistake, and she's

fine, and they hang up.

"Fix it," she turns back to me. "Fix it, fix it."

"Let me get a Band-Aid," I say rising.

"No, not that, that's nothing. I'm talking about the ache." She points to the base of her neck, shouting all the while, until I am at work, curving my hands around her shoulder. She closes her eyes and moans, and I look away. It seems too intimate to witness so much pleasure, and to be the source of it. I am not quite sure what it stirs up in me.

"When did the pain start?" I ask to distract myself.

"About a month ago," she says. "When I called you. It's terrible, growing older, Ava," she says. She is sobbing now. "You don't know what to expect from one day to the next. Nothing stays the same, everything you thought you could count on is snatched out from under your feet, one at a time, in no particular order, no rhyme or reason."

I am still kneading the spot, with the bottom of my palms now. "Nothing to be afraid of," I say. "You got me now, and King." I am still rubbing.

"For now, but you're going to leave. Like today, I looked and looked, and you were nowhere to be found."

"We're not leaving, Grandma." I say. "We're staying right here."

She pauses. "So everything's going to be okay?" she asks, and she sounds like a little girl in a way that makes me want to both reassure her and pull her upright, remind her of her true age.

I'm too uncomfortable not to say something back. "Better than okay," I say.

"You sure, Ava?" She winces all of a sudden.

"Did I hurt you?" I ask. I realize that despite how little she sounds, how powerless, I'm afraid.

"No, the opposite, you got it." She wobbles her head back and forth. "Perfect," she says.

Later, King eats his dinner fast, then asks to be excused. I can hear him from the kitchen talking to the girls on three-way. I take my time clearing the table, then making my old favorite, measuring the Cocchi Americano, the sweet vermouth, even carving out the curl of the lemon peel. I am procrastinating checking on Grandma Martha. She has her nurse who comes by to monitor her bath most nights, but I have been the one to tuck her in since I moved in. Only tonight after her episode — which is still pressing on me

— I'm not sure what I'll find.

When I arrive upstairs, I am relieved to see she's still sleeping away. I head back down to my own room and start to unpack. My great-great-great-grandmother's picture has been in a box since my first week here, and I stare at it for a while. Every time I see it, I notice a new thing; this time it's the fear in her eyes. She wasn't only lonely, she was afraid, of being by herself in a world that she had only started to manage with her husband beside her. I hear a series of creaks above me, footsteps. Grandma was sleeping but she must have woken up. The nurse is up there if she needs anything. I wash my face and take my earrings off, lay them down on the dresser, and sit on the edge of my bed. I am about to lie down when I hear glass breaking, as sharp as if it's my own bedroom mirror that has been busted. I race downstairs and check all the windows but they're secure. I open the front door, and a black boy not much older than King is squatted in the next-door neighbors' driveway, reaching inside their new Lexus SUV. He looks up at me and we lock eyes before he dashes away. The neighbors are out now. They want answers, and they look at me with disdain, like I was the one who caused the scene. After they examine the car, they call the police. It doesn't take long for the officers to arrive and draft a report. One of them asks me if I caught a face, a vague description. I shake my head. "Nothing," I say, and I turn back inside.

The next day I drive King back to the old neighborhood to see his friend. Central City has struggled, and you see it in the empty lots and boarded-up windows, but new restaurants and shops are popping up on O. C. Haley, and of course there are the neighborhood's anchors: Ashé Cultural Arts Center where King and I would go for open mics and drum workshops; Café Reconcile where I'd treat myself on Mondays to red beans and bananas Foster bread pudding. As ready as I was to leave this place, in a way it's a relief to be back, to see the older women sitting on the porches of bright shotguns snapping green beans, the young men kneeling over their front lawns, resuscitating old cars. We reach the apartments and I almost want to pull into my own spot. Crossing the lawn for Senait's front door, we have to bypass flat bags of Lay's potato chips and empty cans of Coke. I know it wasn't Senait. I remember having to wake up every morning and sort through the trash some roamer had left on my stoop the night before.

When we get inside it's just like old times. King grabs red soda and Cheetos from Senait's kitchen and carries them into the back with the kids to watch YouTube videos. I sit at the table while my friend cuts chicken tenders for dinner. She passes me salt and vinegar potato chips and a jar of sliced pickles, and for some reason, telling her I'm not supposed to be eating that stuff makes me feel better about tearing open the bag, sliding my fingers into the juice. As she slices around the chicken fat, she catches me up.

"Sandra's son's girlfriend had the baby, a lil' girl, and they named her Aubrey. She look just like her daddy."

"And Destiny's daddy got out the other week. They had a lil' party for him but I had to work."

"I'm surprised you didn't take off, with his fine ass."

"Girl, you know I tried, but I'm already only four days on, three days off. He ain't worth losing my whole job." She furrows her brow, like she's considering what she just said. "At least I don't think he is."

We laugh.

"I miss you," I say.

"Please, you got the maid and the butler and the cook."

"I'm not gon' lie, Binh can show you how to fry some chicken. He can show your mama too. I brought you some of his *yaka mein.*" I pat the Tupperware in my tote.

I pause. "I don't know though. My grand-mother, she's family and all that, but it's weird, living in somebody else's house. And King's the only black kid in his class. I don't want him to become all golly gee."

"Not golly gee. What the hell is *golly gee?*"

"You remember Carlton from *The Fresh Prince?*"

I stand up and start snapping my fingers, switching my hips, and she laughs.

"Seriously though, it might affect his self-esteem," I say, sitting down.

"Self-esteem? I know you doing fine if you talking about self-esteem."

"You saw the news?" she asks.

I nod. Two boys King's age had been shot around the corner a few nights ago. One of them had died and the other one was hang-ing on at Ochsner Hospital.

"He's going to live," she goes on, "but that's the worst part. They got him in the brain. He won't be able to dress himself again. At least they didn't kill him." She shakes her head.

"You know I don't like to be negative. I'm only bringing that up so you remember, you lucky you got King out of here," she says.

I know that. "I'm grateful," I say. I almost don't say the next part. It seems extravagant, but I'm not as comfortable as I hoped I'd be, as I was that first night.

I pause again, then go on. "And then he hangs out with these white girls," I say.

She looks up at that. "Not white girls."

"Yeah, white girls. Claire and Harper."

"Hmph." She is dipping the chicken in egg yolks, then flour. When the pieces hit the pan the grease pops and sizzles. "You might want to watch that," she says.

"I know," I say. "That's why I brought it up. I am."

"Ain't too long before they're acting like he's coming on to them or something."

I shake my head. "Then again, the mothers are really nice. They came up and introduced themselves the other day. They were singing and —"

"Yeah, they're nice today," she cuts me off, "singing off-key and shit, but you better believe they're watching, and if he even hugs those lil' girls too hard."

"Maybe you're right."

"Ain't no *maybe* about it."

I can see the chicken skin browning.

"You just be careful, girl. You don't want to be going from one kind of danger to another."

King walks into the kitchen and sits at the table beside me, takes out his phone.

"Aren't you supposed to be playing with Nathan?" I ask.

"They don't say *playing,* Mom," he says, but he doesn't budge either. For the rest of the time I'm there, he's right next to me, and he only nods at his friend when it's time to leave.

On the way back, I prod him for answers — he had been the one begging me to go to Senait's — but he just offers up that middle school silence, so I let it go.

My mother calls when I get home. She's in a good mood, says she had a doctor's appointment in the area, and wants to stop by and see the new place.

"Of course," I say. Ordinarily, I'd be hesitant, but lately it's just been me and Grandma and I could use somebody else, even if it is my mother. I sit with Grandma until her nap, then I straighten up the pillows on the sofa, dust the shelves, vacuum the rugs though there is nothing on them.

Still I am embarrassed at what my mother will see, the pictures of old white people on every wall. They are stern and unrelenting in their eyes, and I wonder for the first time how they'd feel about me eating off their china. I remember my great-great-great-grandmother upstairs and hurry for the frame. It is hard to know where to place her, but I choose an end table in the corner. You'd only see her there if you were looking, but once you found her, you wouldn't misplace her again.

My mother is smiling when I open the door. I lead her in and she walks from one end of the living room to the other. She's been here before and she doesn't seem as awed as King was. She finds Josephine's picture immediately and moves her hand out to touch it then pulls it back like something might bite her.

King comes bounding down the stairs.

"There's my boy," she says. She hugs him, then she reaches into her pocketbook for a tin can. Pralines. "I just made them," she sings. "I think they've cooled."

We sit down on the sofa, then he fishes for the biggest piece, takes a bite.

"Yooo." He closes his eyes. "Yooo, Maw Maw, this is out of this world. This is better than the praline man that sells them for a dollar outside my old school. You could sell these, you know."

She nods. "I know. None of that devil dairy in there either," she says.

"You don't miss it neither," King says, reaching for another one.

She fidgets in her seat, still looking around. "So what, is it a holiday I didn't know about?"

"Parent–teacher appreciation," I say back.

"Um-hmm, seem like the better the school is, the less time they actually have you in there."

King and I laugh.

"You liking it though, King?"

"Yes, ma'am."

"You don't just have to say that 'cause your mama's here now." She's smiling though. "You know you tell Maw Maw the truth. You miss your old friends?"

"We just got back from Senait's," I say.

"I know you were glad to see Nathan," my mother says.

King shrugs. "He didn't have that much to say to me," he says.

King's about to say something more when I hear the slow drag of Grandma approaching. I turn.

"Grandma," I say, "I didn't hear you get up."

"You don't eat in this part of the house," she snaps. Her voice is shrill and hard. King covers the top of the tin.

She looks around in a panic. I can tell she's having trouble orienting herself. Then her attention fixes on something and I look over to see that it's the picture in the corner that I just propped up, the one of Josephine.

"Grandma," I say, "you remember my mother. She just wanted to come by and see where we've been staying."

My mother stands up to greet her.

Grandma seems like she's still out of it but she zeroes in on my mother's face and comes to.

"Oh, you must have found the secret of youth, Gladys," she says after only a little while.

My mother smiles but it is not her normal smile. "Likewise," she says.

"Oh, you don't have to lie," Grandma says. "What's your secret?" She leans in. "Really, tell me," she whispers.

"Water and coconut oil and minding my own goddamn business," my mother says. She is still smiling that half smile. I've seen it before, when she'd talk with white teachers at my school who said I was doing my best though I'd only earned a C in the class. Or at the grocery store when a cashier gave attention to someone behind her first. It was the smile she wore when she was about to pounce.

"Well, she *tries* to mind her own business," I say, and I feel the tension settle. Even my mother laughs.

"Go get her some tea." Grandma Martha nods in my direction and I get up and boil some water. When I'm back in the room, Grandma and Mama are sitting next to each other on the sofa. King has gone upstairs, and the women are talking like contemporaries. My mother seems more comfortable when I hand her her cup, sharing that her life changed when she decided to become a doula. She wakes up, she says, thinking about her girls. She goes to sleep thinking about them. They give her purpose.

"Oh, yes," Grandma says. "I know all about that. When Ava's daddy went off to school I started tutoring the neighborhood kids. Just a few blocks away but life couldn't be more different. Some of them didn't even know what sounds their letters made, or their numbers one through ten. Can you imagine? Five years old, but I'd get a slate and a piece of chalk the same way my mother taught me, and after a few months, they'd be reading Laura Ingalls Wilder."

"Well, bless your heart," my mother says.

"That's right," Grandma sings.

Binh comes out and says dinner is ready and Grandma tells him to prepare an extra plate. My mother looks at me, and I nod and call upstairs for King, and we all walk over to the table. It has been set like always with a fall floral arrangement of orange and gold in the center. The place mats are crisp and the silverware is gathered and clasped in cloth. I look over at my mother with concern — I don't remember her ever eating with my grandmother — but she doesn't seem out of place.

Grandma Martha talks through dinner, circling around the same old stories.

"When I was a little girl, nothing but a snatch of a thing, the boys would ride over and they'd rattle their tails around our porch. Daddy called us the Dufrene girls, and everybody wanted a piece of us, I tell you. From the time we were thirteen they wanted to see what was under our petticoats, and the funny thing was sometimes we showed them."

King is used to it and just sops up his corn chowder with his sourdough roll. I glance at my mother throughout the monologue and I notice she doesn't eat the food, just spreads it around her bowl. At first she is quick with the polite *um-hmm*s and the *Is* *that so*s, but after a while even the superficial conversation subsides. The more Grandma talks, the more tired my mother seems, and by the end, I have to help her out of her seat.

We return to the parlor after dinner. King joins us, and we are about to walk my mother out when King's phone rings. It's a FaceTime call, and Harper's face flashes across the screen for a minute, then he hangs up. Before we can stand, Grandma pipes up.

"King, who's that you were sitting next to?"

I look over at my son. He is alone on the sofa. I look at my mother.

"That little blond cherub, young, but what a beauty," Grandma goes on. "You sure you supposed to be talking to her this time of night?" she asks, her voice upturned.

"It's not that late, Grandma," I say.

"Yeah, but what would her father say?" she asks. "A big boy like you talking to that little old thing. You have to ask yourself how it appears —"

"Grandma," I stop her. "That's enough," I say. I pause. "You must be tired."

I walk over. Juanita is already running her bath when we reach her room, and I explain that Grandma had a long day.

I am embarrassed at what she said, and the whole way back downstairs, I'm preparing my excuses, but my mother is already at the door. She seems unsteady on the walk to her car and I offer to drive her home, but she refuses. She doesn't mention Grandma's outburst.

"Call me when you get back," I make her promise, and she kisses me on the cheek.

I go back inside and I hear Grandma whistling from the kitchen: "Amazing Grace." I don't know how she made it back down so fast. Not only that, but she is standing, shifting dishes from the counter to the sink quicker than I've seen her move since I arrived. I try to stop her but she puts her hand up in my face.

"No, no," she says. "Let me; it's rare, but nothing feels better than getting back to my old self. I think I need to see my friends more. Spending time with your mother really brought me back to life. I used to host parties, played bridge every other Sunday. I'd prepare a big spread, chicken salad and croissants, petit fours, you name it."

She is humming now too, and when the dishes are cleared, she is on to the countertops, wiping them with bleach until they shine. She wants to walk upstairs by herself and I let her. Still, I double-check to make sure she hasn't turned on the burners by mistake and that all the food is put away. But no, everything is secure. My mother texts me. She is home. She was tired from giving blood earlier is all.

I walk back to the living room and try to see the place the way she would have seen it. No doubt it is impressive, but it is not mine. And then Grandma Martha's comments toward King. If anybody else had said them, I would have cursed her out, point-blank. It's Grandma though, and of course she didn't mean anything by it. That's what I would have told my mother if she had stuck around. I wonder if she had even taken in the photograph. I walk toward the corner for it, and it's not where I left it. I look around the whole living room, ask King but he says he hasn't seen it either. I start to bother Grandma Martha, but something tells me to check my own room first. There it is, on my bed. I know I didn't, but I must have moved it and forgotten.

JOSEPHINE

1924

Most boys Jericho's age still work the fields; they go to school in the fall after the cotton is picked, but come spring, planting season, they are out again. Their parents have as many children as they can, call them hands because each one signifies a set of two, but I see to it that Jericho attends school year-round. His father grunts, tickled all the while that the boy can read the book of Psalms by himself.

When Jericho is off, and I've had my morning grits and bacon, I set to my own work. It has been many years since I mid-wifed regularly, or nursed a white woman's baby, but I still wash the clothes, haul the water, tend the fire, change the linen, dust, cook, preserve. I tried to eat lunch with the workers at first, but I feel useless sitting, knowing they will toss a sandwich back in one hand and spray the aphids off the orchard leaves with the other. There is a table I set up when I moved here to bring my mother back, an altar that I covered in her favorite blue cloth, the sage she burned, and stones she carried. But I hung my head over it, I prayed and prayed, I chanted and I sang, and she never returned.

I am rising from my morning nap when I hear the knock.

I figure it is Theron, the farmhand. Isaiah used to work the land for Mr. Dennis like the others. We lived in a cabin down the row, and every month we received our share minus debt payments. Then Mr. Dennis took to drinking, and with the drinking came the gambling, and in a desperate month he offered all the sharecroppers two acres for $50. My husband had lucked on a turning plow a few years earlier and was yielding more crops than he owed. I'd ride to market to sell them for him, and as a result, he was the only one who had the money. That two acres stretched to four, then ten, then fifteen, and after five years, Mr. Dennis was in the ground and my Isaiah was on top of it. Now since Isaiah's death, Theron tends. He comes by if some of the corn stalks produce small ears, or the greens have wilted, but I look through the tiny circle drilled into the door and it is not him. No, it's just that white woman from yesterday, Sarah or Scarlett, I'm not sure I care which.

"Good day. Can I help you?" I open the door an inch and peer through a crack.

"Yes, ma'am, I just came to offer you a jar of jam. I made it last week. I'm trying to have a baby you see, and my mama wrote me and said the more I act like a mother the more God will get the picture, so I'm pruning and canning and ironing and washing as if I got a house full of kids, and it ain't but me and my husband, so it all just goes to waste." She pauses then, and for the first time looks up in my eyes. Hers are big as dresser knobs, blue too. I know some people find them beautiful. Still she carries an odor, seems intended, like she sprayed rose water between her legs but the flowers had died, and I step back.

"I saw your little boy with you the other day is the thing. Seems like maybe he might be interested."

I laugh, not just laugh but holler. People stand in line for my jam; they compete over who can bring me the most berries come their respective season; they find me the largest jars so I can carry out their orders first; when I'm done, they open the jar at my table, long before they reach home because they've been dreaming about the way the sweet melds into the tart, the way the juice creams; they poke fingers into the fruit because they can't wait until the bread is sliced; they don't just spread it on bread, they spoon it into beans and rice or potato salad because they can't leave a good thing alone. So I lean my head back and let my body shake, let my tongue flick out and my jaws collapse on themselves.

"What's so funny?" she asks.

I shrug. Let her wonder.

"I was just being neighborly." She seems embarrassed now and maybe I feel a little guilty. Not any more than a touch.

"Why don't you come on in?" I say.

She seems to sigh and stays by the door.

"Suit yourself," I say, and let the door swing back on its hinges, but she catches it and steps inside.

"It's so clean in here." She follows close behind me like she might get lost if she's off a step.

"Yeah, that's how I keep it," I say.

"And it smells so good. Smells like you were baking bread."

"Always got some on."

"That'll go nice with this." She pats the jar in her arms, and I roll my eyes.

"Care for some coffee?"

"Tea would be better."

I fix her a cup and we sit. "So you and your husband aiming to be in the family way," I say more than ask.

She nods. She doesn't seem like too much more than a child herself, stringy hair, gap in her teeth, scrawny like she doesn't get enough cow's milk. I have five cows out back, and we eat cream in our eggs every morning. If she was one of mine, I'd get up and scramble her some.

"I had three children, two girls, one boy. Only one of them is with me now. Trust me, the more girls you have, the better. When I was pregnant with my first daughter, my own mama came to me in a dream, said, this girl inside you is going to be your friend. And that's how it was. Three years old, giving me advice about her father. I'll never forget that, told me I needed to communicate how I was feeling, otherwise he wouldn't know. It was simple, simple as a child, but it changed things for me, let me tell you that." I look up. I have no idea why I've been rambling so.

"Where is she now?" she asks.

"Who?"

"Your oldest daughter."

"Oh, she followed her husband up north. He had people up there and big dreams. He was always a dreamer. If they were catching fish, he wanted the trout; if they were riding in a carriage, he was fiending for baling wire to repair the Model T Ford. I was there when he was born, see, one of the other sharecropper's sons. They've been sweet on each other since they were at the breast. What could I tell her? Stay here? I miss her every day, but I'm glad she didn't settle."

She pushes the jar of jam over to me. "Try some," she says. She is so proud I twist open the top. I move to slide my bread out of the oven, carry it over, slice it where the steam still rises, pass her some, watch her spread her concoction across the cooked dough. I don't need to taste it to know her contribution is subpar, loose where it should be tight, spare where it should burst forth.

She gasps from her first bite. "This bread, it's divine, it's heavenly. I barely taste the jam with the bread like this against it."

Well, she said it. I eat around the dark red mass. That bread is good, some of my best, and I ooh and aah over the creation, vague enough so she doesn't know what I am complimenting, and she doesn't see that I throw the majority of her goo out to the pigs. She doesn't leave a crumb on her plate.

I peel back the white curtain shielding my kitchen window and peek through it, see

Major leading Aristide Taylor toward the door. Major has started dressing fancier since he met Eliza. Though he runs the fields, today he is wearing a hat, vest, jacket, and trousers held up by suspenders. Aristide used to sharecrop too, but he owns the farm west of ours now. Just a little plot of land, but it's something. I don't know why they're coming, but Carla, or whatever, would have to leave. I move toward the door.

"Thank you so kindly for the jam," I say.

"It was my pleasure." She is still sitting though. "Jam always tastes better when you can share it," she says. "I reckon all food is like that. I was intending to make some biscuits tomorrow. Maybe I can come by and share a dozen. If they come out right, that is. I ain't never made them alone; normally my mama is right there standing over me, so they could forget to rise in the oven for all I know."

"Sure," I say just to shut her up. "That'd be real nice."

"It's a date then." She stands, and crumbs fall off her skirt and hit the floor. "I'm so sorry." She kneels down to pick them up.

"Don't worry about it." I almost grab her hand, and on second thought just gesture toward it, then toward the door, hoping she'll connect the two motions and see her way out.

When I open up, the men walk straight in. Their shoulders are touching, but they are steady arguing.

The white woman looks from me to them several times but she still won't budge.

"This is my son, Major, and Aristide Taylor," I tell her because I still can't be sure what her name is.

"Charlotte," she says, holding her hand out.

"She lives next door. She was just leaving." She is barely over the threshold when I close the door. I turn to offer the men lemonade, but they don't even hear me.

"You know I respect your daddy, but that cotton you aiming to sell is picked right off my property," Aristide is in the middle of shouting. He's a big man and when he talks he settles his hands on the tip of his belly.

"Now, we been over this before, Aristide," Major interrupts him.

"I know what happened last time and I'm mighty sorry, but you better check again. This time I'm certain."

Soon as I hear the fuss is about land, I move for the deed. Disputes like this come up from time to time, and Isaiah taught me it's better to let the paper do the talking. I skim it before I bring it in. Major is looking at me while I walk, and before I can tell him what it says, he snatches it from me.

I can see the gist of it from his face, which falls. He is embarrassed to be wrong, embarrassed because his father never was.

"All right, you right. I reckon some of it's on yours," he says.

"I told you I was right, boy." This from Aristide.

"Well, all right, I'll give you half my earnings from it, then."

"Don't want half your earnings, I want the crop itself."

"Hell no, you ain't getting no crop."

"Watch your mouth, Major," I say.

"Half the earnings and that's that," he repeats.

Aristide pauses. "Your daddy never woulda done it that way," he says. That is the worst thing anybody could have told Major, and wrong as I think my son is, I wish Aristide hadn't said it.

Major has been knocked off his footing now and it takes him a while to gather his thoughts again.

"It's getting late, Aristide. Why don't we just talk about this later?" I walk him toward the door.

"That's fine, Josephine, but I'm telling you, you know I love you, loved your husband, but that boy of yours ain't right about that cotton."

"I hear you, Aristide," I say, "but let's talk about it tomorrow," and he repeats himself two more times before I can shut the door.

I turn back to Major. He is at the table now, sitting with his head in his hands.

"You think I'm wrong, Mama? You can say it if you do."

I sit across from him. "It's a complicated issue, son. Your daddy always followed his instinct. He said it was the same as following his heart, and his heart always told him to treat black people better than he would have wanted to be treated. There was the golden rule and there was Isaiah's rule, remember that?"

Major laughs. "Yeah, I remember." His face hardens fast. "The thing is, Aristide don't respect me, none of them do, and if I don't put my foot down now, they never will."

I don't say a word. Major has always been the most literal child. I'd have to give him reams of instructions for a simple task. To my daughters I could say, go get ready for the day, and they'd know to wash their face, brush their teeth, pull on their skirts, make up their beds, but I'd spell out every step for Major: walk to the bedroom, open the

115

dresser, dig through for a shirt. Another thing is, he's easily influenced. I called him Major to protect him. A white man referencing him would have to extend him respect, whether he meant to or not, just by virtue of saying his name. Still I had so much trouble with him when he was younger because he'd let boys with no hair on their chest explain to him how to be a man. It was hard enough before his father died, but then with Isaiah gone my job doubled. I'd forget about my grief most nights, I'd go to bed with worry skating across my heart, worry over Major. Even now, if it was one of my daughters, namely my oldest, all I'd have to say is *Don't confuse weakness with strength. You want somebody to do something for you, you bend over backwards to do it for them.* That is how it goes with respect. But Major wouldn't understand that, so I just rub his back and it heaves under my palm. He is not crying the way he would when he was a young boy, but this is the closest he can get to it.

He stays for dinner that night. Jericho and Theron come over and I suggest a game of cards to get our mind off Aristide and his cotton. When we're halfway through one round, the ribbing starts.

"I'm thinking about going to see my

116

brother down south next month," I say to Major.

"You ain't got no brother, Josephine, stop all that cheating now," Theron snaps back.

"No, no, I'm not cheating, brother. I just want to say that my brother got a bad heart, real bad heart, and I'm gon' see about him."

"I done said that's enough of that," Theron says, but he is grinning. He is a slight man and even his smiles seem to come out in a whisper.

He bids a five, calling spades, and I raise my eyebrows. My own hand wouldn't have warranted it.

Major and I bid a three and four and Theron leads off with a spade.

"All that mess you was talking in the beginning about your brother." Theron pokes a finger in his hunk of coconut cake and swivels off a piece of icing, jabs it in his mouth.

"Oh, please, I wouldn't have had to say a word. We been whippin' y'all behinds since we started partnering up. Just last week we ran a Boston."

"On who?"

Jericho adds a spade, then Major.

"We ran one."

Then I play an ace and it's my hand.

"You ain't ran one on us. We what and

what now."

I lead out with an ace in trump and Major is right behind me with a joker.

I call a diamond then, knowing Theron doesn't have a single one. He tries to tell Jericho by throwing out a ten of clubs but Jericho is just learning; he keeps on with the diamonds and Theron lays down his final high club.

Major goes before me this time with an ace of diamonds, and winks at me.

I lay the joker down and Theron rises to his feet hot. "You cheating with him," he starts. "You cheating with him."

And the whole while we are shouting we are laughing. It is like old times I tell you, and the men are drinking whiskey and half the cake is gone, and I intend for it all to be eaten tonight. I start to deal again, but before I can get my hand steady, Major says he has to get back.

"Eliza waiting on me is the thing. I got to get back, see about her." He stands. I watch Jericho lick his fork clean, then cut another sliver straight from the platter, haul back a glass of milk. I expect him to head back to my room now to get changed for the night but he walks to the front door behind his daddy.

I don't have the sense to hide my hurt.

"You leaving?" I ask like a woman half my age. "Okay, no problem," I say. "No problem," I repeat. I walk to the door and see them off, waving all the while. I take my time with the dishes. There isn't anything on the other side of the chore waiting for me. I had made a plate for Eliza. Heaping piles of potatoes and okra and I am regretting it now. Some people get so much.

The next day the white woman is back. I know it is her because of the timid way she knocks like maybe she is at the wrong house after all. She has caught me again right after my nap and my hair is everywhere so I tie on a scarf before I hurry to the door.

"Can I help you with something?" I ask, holding the door to my body like there's something I don't want her to see.

"You remember our date?" she asks me.

"Date?" I ask.

She laughs, a little giggle, and there is something about that silly spurt of a sound that makes me want to pull my shoulders back.

"I guess that's not the right word, but I was just being funny. You remember yesterday? I told you I'd bring the biscuits by if they came out all right? And they came out fine. Nothing like your bread of course, but better than my mama's. She never was such a good cook to say she did it so often. Whenever I think about her she's standing in front of a stove. Ain't that sad? Every memory I have of my mama finds her with her back to me, hunched over. I think that's sad," she says when I don't answer.

She moves while she talks. She can't stay still, can't stay silent neither. It's not that she says anything strange, just too much, like she doesn't know the ways of the world.

"She was taking care of you all," I say. The door shifts back a little.

"I'm just going on and on," she says, "and I haven't even offered you a taste. Would you like to try them?"

"Sure." I let my grip on the door loosen, just enough for her to slide in. I don't want her there, and I do. It was nice to have company yesterday, but I am not stupid. I know who she is, who I am in comparison.

She sits down and I pull out the plates, just like the other day. Just like the other day, I dread having to taste her food.

"Seemed like there was a disagreement yesterday. Did you sort it out?"

"It will get sorted."

"Land issue, huh? It's amazing to me how riled up people get about it. It's not a living thing, it's not breathing, but people give it all this power."

121

I shrug. Receiving it sure seemed powerful to us.

"You find it hard not going somewhere, doing something, day after day?" she goes on. "If I had a child, there would be something occupying me. But as it is, I just float around from one empty corner of the room to the next. Sometimes when my husband leaves, I want to jump into his coat pocket, beg him to take me with him."

If she had hit me with that ten years ago, even five, the words would have been incomprehensible to me, white people jibber jabber. I might have nodded and smiled thinking, *Bless her heart.* And I'm not saying I respect it today. But I empathize. Old age has been the biggest shock of my life. I don't have any models for how to live it out right. My own mama taught me how to clean between my legs, to fry fish in a lean fire.

But nobody taught me how to sit down.

I slice a biscuit for her, then me, half because I don't eat white people's food. Never had the occasion to and don't intend to start now, but manners are manners and right is right. I have to admit the biscuits are a sandy brown, and wispy on the inside. I pick a bite off and place it on my tongue. A grunt of surprise catches in my throat.

"You say you used your mama's recipe for this?"

"Yes, ma'am," she nods. "Did it turn out all right? Sometimes I forget the little things, vanilla, or once I mistook salt for sugar, didn't catch the mistake until the first bite." She giggles again. "What did I miss here?"

I take another bite. I am almost done with my share. If it was Link's biscuits tasting like this, I'd have devoured half a dozen by now.

"It's not bad," I say.

She looks down at her lap, like a little child who was hoping for an orange and got a lemon.

"It's not bad at all," I add. "In fact, they're the best biscuits I ever tasted."

She just lights up at that, Christmas morning and birthday pie all rolled into one.

"There's something I been meaning to ask you," she says.

"What is it?" She catches me off guard though I can't have the nerve to be surprised. White women don't sniff around black women's kitchens too long before they set their sights on something they can take, something they have got to have.

"There's a rumor going around about you. My husband's the one who put me on

123

it. He said you're some kind of conjure woman, said everybody around these parts knows about it, said a lot of the people who come in and out here are coming for that reason."

I pause. It is the strangest thing — the moments that call me to miss my daughters can't be timed. I had been close to them both, but it was the oldest whom I thought would be my forever child. I had to press her small body to mine the first time she used the outhouse, she was so afraid to try new things. She learned to beat the white women's clothes with sticks, fold them, then carry them in wheelbarrows for me when she was three 'cause she didn't want to leave my side. She slept with me every night after her father passed, and she would have stayed too, but her husband was itching for a way out of Jim Crow, and his brother was moving to Philadelphia, and what could I say? She writes me every week, and she is happy with her two children. I would have liked to hold them just once, but what else can I want for her?

"Hmph. I could water my entire farm with the lies people tell," I say.

"It wouldn't be the first time my husband got something wrong. Don't tell him I said that."

"I won't say a word," I say, and we both laugh.

" 'Cause if he was right, I was going to ask you about the baby. If you could put one inside me."

Here we go.

I don't say a word, just stare back at her, transfer some of the discomfort she lit up in me right back over to her. Sure, used to be, there was a time when I could say yes. When I first got here, to bind my mother to me, I unfolded a picture of her from my breast pocket, laid it out over my prayer table, along with her pearl comb. I burned sage and dressed a blue candle in sweet oil. Wasn't just that: people came from all over to relieve the weight of their hearts. Most times I didn't say a word, just sat there, listened to them wail about their daughter's face, snatched just before the war, and they couldn't call it up any longer; or guilt, and the more of it there was, the worse things people did to snuff it out. The whole while I was writing out prayers on their behalf I was standing over a pot of my mother's favorite, stewed gizzards; I was nurturing visions of her every morning, chanting her name like jewels on a necklace, but Link came back more than once with an empty hand, and the last time, the very last time I had her search, I burned all the sage, the cloth, the comb. I couldn't bring myself to destroy her image, but it sits at the back of my dresser now, and I'm too carved out to pick it up.

"But you said you don't do that sort of thing," the white woman repeats herself.

"No indeed," I say, and I don't say another word more. For a little while we sit like that, her looking up, then back down at her lap, and me just staring straight at her like there's a picture show across her face, and I'm more entertained than I've been in some time, wondering how long the silence can go.

"Ooh, I've got to get supper," I say after a while, but she still doesn't leave. Since she's there, I pass her the bowl of green beans, have her snap each one at both ends. It gets done quicker that way.

While she snaps she tells me things, things I might have reserved for a friend: that she didn't know her husband that well when they met, but that her mama said that he wore nice shoes, that his mama had all her teeth. The wedding had been half a celebration, a small cake and her daddy gave a toast, but there were only a few people there, her husband being from such a small family and her own people unable to pay

126

for much more than potato salad and a chicken to fry.

"I'm not saying my parents did me wrong, we made do," she says. "We made do, but it's nothing like it is here. All the corn and sweet potatoes and cabbage I could eat. My mama visits me and I long to see her, but it hurts too; everything she's seeing, it's good for me, but I can tell she's shrinking. I thought I'd make her proud but I've noticed shame there too."

"No, girl," I say, thinking of my own children. "Nothing about you is cause for shame. Kill a man, steal a child, now that's shameful. Your mama is proud of you, she just wants more for herself, that's all."

You can have both things. One doesn't ride the other one out.

That seems to hit her deep somewhere and stick; she thinks on it for a while.

"What about you?" she asks. "You close with your daughters who are gone?"

"Couldn't be closer," I say without thinking. "Even if they were here. They write me so much, I feel like I'm in the room with them sometimes. Send pictures too. I got grandchildren, three already and one on the way. One of them is named after me. Josephyne. Spelled with a *y* instead of an *i*. But it's after me."

"You miss 'em though? The ones you don't have with you?"

I feel myself shaking inside some mornings so hard I can't even hold my spoon steady, and having her name the wound brings heat to it, but I just sit there.

"Sometimes," I say, snapping away at those beans. When the last is broken, and there is no use for my hands, I set them against the table, one over the other to hold them back. "Sometimes it's more than I can bear," I have to say.

The thing is, no matter how old you get, you still imagine them as your babies. I can still see the first one not five minutes after she was born, puckering her lips at me. She didn't know what world she had landed in or how she got there, what her role in it would be, but she knew she needed to eat, and I was the one who could provide. I look up then. I can feel some water on my cheek, the tip of it.

"You'll see," I say.

She shrugs. "I'm beginning to lose hope."

"How long has it been?"

"Two years."

I try not to let my concern show. Anyway I have seen worse. "And you've been having regular relations all that time?"

She nods. "Every day almost. At this point

we would need a miracle," she laughs.

"Well, don't cut your eyes at a miracle; miracles are more everyday than people think. You know how your eyes work? How you set your mind on stepping out of bed and walking and your legs just follow suit?" She shrugs.

"I don't. What's a miracle? Something you can't explain coming to pass; something that doesn't make sense existing anyway. So much of the day is miraculous. And if you notice one example, you'll get pointed in the direction of another. The insides of them, that buzz, that fire, will fill you up inside and you can put your hand out and touch something commonplace and watch it bloom into something else that shouldn't be. There's the stuff of miracles swimming all inside you, all around you, you just haven't reached in and grabbed it yet."

"That's beautiful," she says.

"Okay."

She looks out the window. "There's one," she says, pointing.

It's a bluebird on a perch just outside my kitchen window, and she is grinning like an idiot.

"Sure is," I say. The moment has passed though. I believe everything I've just said, it is my ministry to teach it, but I feel like I've lost something sharing it with her. There was a cost to that truth, the buds of which didn't form until I fled Wildwood, and if I hadn't met Isaiah, Lord knows what would have come of me. Before I looked across a planter's field of cotton at him, I'd get still in the bottom of myself, and blocks of words would show up in my mind's eye: *The harder the harvest, the more robust the fruit.* In the mornings, just before daybreak, with my eyes only half open, I'd see that woman that comes to me, young and supple still, and I wouldn't be able to understand her words, but seeing her face would feel like my mother's hand stretched over my heart. I'd wake up knowing no matter what the day held, I'd already passed through it.

There were other things, and now the quieter I am, the more verdant my life, the more green and lush, and giving away my yield to this woman feels like taking it from my Maker, the opposite of gratitude, and a sure way to confuse the Source. She is still going on about the sun and the breeze when her face hardens.

"Lord, that's Vern," she says. "I gotta go," and she almost stumbles she scrambles out of my chair so fast. It is no matter. The beans are snapped. I'd smother some potatoes, and by the time I'd be done, maybe

Jericho would be coming to eat dinner. But time wears on and he just isn't there. And the longer I sit there, the longer I feel like I have been plucked clear of anything decent that was inside me and there is only one place to go to get stuffed back up.

Link lives where the sharecroppers did, a quarter of a mile downhill from me, just the time it takes me to forget the empty way I felt sitting at that table in the white woman's wake. It is still daylight, and the sun covers me on all sides. There are small clusters of unpainted houses along the way with wood frames and swinging windows, hog yards and vegetable gardens closed in by chicken wire. When I reach Link's, I can feel the dampness under the sleeves of my dress, and I have to take out my handkerchief and wipe the beads gathering on my forehead.

She is outside looking beyond her porch like she was expecting me, her door open behind her. I can glimpse two baby pictures of her son hanging on the nearest wall, surrounded by newspaper to seal the gaps in the rough-hewn boards.

"Hey, you," she calls out.

I wave at her. "What you up to?"

"Thinking of making pillowcases but ran out of cloth."

"We could see what the pastor's wife is

holding," I say, and she stands, grips the rails on either side of her stairs, then, slower than I would on account of her toes missing, climbs down the four steps. When she reaches the bottom, we start the trek to church. Two boys to our right kneel to work on a car. Several feet ahead of us, my old neighbor rides a mule-drawn wagon weighed down by sacks of cotton. He looks back and waves.

"Good afternoon, Josephine, Link."

"All right now," we say back, our greetings merged.

Link tells me about her crops: "Corn's failing, fifteen bushels per acre. When last year it was twenty. It's hard to fight the slugs these days, but I got more tomatoes than anything. If I can sell those, I'll be all right."

"That's nice," I say, or maybe I don't say it; maybe I just think it. Then we hear the toll of the bell sounding from the direction we're moving in, and we pick up our speed. We don't speak the whole way. The thing is the bell is almost never a surprise like it is now. Word creeps around that someone is sick and shut in and a few weeks later, the confirmation will sound from the church's slight steeple, but we will have minded that progression, with pans of barbecue and jugs of milk and baskets of eggs. In this case, the clang hasn't stopped and I don't know what to expect.

I rush up to the front steps, and Link is a lick behind me. When I see Aristide's son, I almost yelp I'm so relieved.

"Paul, you back?" I ask. I look closer at him. He is much smaller than he was when he left and he leans on a stick for balance.

Link is on my heels, and when she sees him, she grabs him by the shoulder but he stares back at her in a daze.

"When you got back?" she asks.

He doesn't answer her until she asks him again.

"When you got back?"

"A little bit ago," he says. "Not too long ago," he repeats.

Link has a fire in her eyes I haven't seen in a while. I look back and forth between her and Paul, my brow furrowing. And then it hits me, that Aristide's boy with the limp had been taken up in the gangs around the same time her Henry had. I can see her determining how to ask the next question, wanting to hurl it at him but needing to be kind too, and when it comes down to it, she can't hold it in.

"And Henry?" she asks. "You seen him?"

Paul shakes his head and looks away like he's recalling something unpleasant to him.

133

"Just in the beginning and then I was able to work out." He looks away again.

She covers her mouth and dips, and I grab her arm.

I look at Paul and ask him with my eyes if there's something more he knows, something he can tell just me alone, and I see behind them, a rot.

"All right now, Link," I say. "All right now. You all right, son?" I ask, and he nods. "Eating all right, and got money to spend?"

He looks down at his feet. His hair is clumped in patches, and he has bumps at the edges of his scalp that rise in clusters.

Aristide approaches.

"Miss Josephine, I was gonna come around there and ask you if Paul could have some land to work. I was gon' do it proper, but since I'm seeing you here, you got something for him? Maybe to get his mind right?"

We got all the hands we could use. Major is running the farm now and he is strict about how much work is distributed. Besides, this boy looks like whatever they had him doing in that gang halved him and I would be getting the dimmest piece. Maybe that's more reason to take him. I look at Link. She got about two seconds before she falls onto this ground.

"Of course, son," I say, "you come by tomorrow." Then I bid the young man farewell and turn back to Link. We had intended to see about the cloth, but it is clear we won't be going anywhere. She doesn't say a word until we near my house. The tallest oak marks the cross between the road that leads to the workers' row and the road to town. Mama always said any cross-road was a meeting between this world and the spirit one. That oak is where I come to clear my mind, and now the corn stalks in its path are moving so fast it's like they were waiting on me. Maybe the movement calms Link down, maybe it stirs her up, but she is waving her arms and stamping her feet. Someone farther from us could think she was dancing.

"If I had known it was going to hurt like this, I would never have had him," she says.

"It's all right, one way or another, it's going to be all right." I rub her back.

We stand like that for a while, her crying into her hands and me holding her.

"Is it?" she asks when she's cleaned her face. "Is it gon' be all right hurting like this?"

"It's gon' hurt for a while."

She pauses before she asks the next question. "There ain't nothing you can do to speed it up?"

I think for a minute. If it was anybody else, I'd tell them, *Sprinkle salt all around the house; let it sit for seven days; then sweep it up and say a prayer over it before you haul it in the fire.* And I would hope it would work, pray for that. But this is Link. And Henry is her son. I don't believe in that stuff anymore. Good bit it did my mother. Good bit it did me. And even when it does work, that hurt doesn't disappear with the salt, it just disperses, to the tips of your fingers, to the base of your heart, to the core of your stomach, and even the hardest woman can't keep it down. Alcohol will surface it, or a sleepless night. Then one fast word from a child, or twisted look from a friend, and that rage is gnarled now, monstrous, unyielding.

"I can sit with you tonight," I say. Everything she's feeling will be divided in half the longer I sit with her.

She rests her face in her hands. "I couldn't ask you that."

"As much as you seen me through," I start.

"Not really, you're strong, Josephine," she says.

I pause. "On account of how much people seen me through," I repeat.

JOSEPHINE

1855

The Revisioners met every Sunday after market, our feet cracked and peeling from bartering poultry, horseshoes, or wood bowls along the levee. At some plantations Mama would only nod at the slaves and at some she would hum a song — she didn't speak the words but I knew them.

It's true they cannot catch me.
There is a schooner out at sea.
It's true they cannot catch me.

The people she sang for would appear in the swamp that night, three hundred yards past the point where the last cabin crossed with the sugarhouse. Eighteen of us gathered in the dark. We sat around an altar covered in blue cloth, milk and sugar, corn, jars of water, a pot of sage, melon seeds, and scraps of pork we snuck from supper.

137

My mama would walk a circle counter-clockwise around us, directing our prayers and lamentations.

"They sold my baby over the river," or "My husband took sick and it won't be much longer," or "My child in trouble and I got to throw up my hands," until our grief was ripe for healing, and our hearts were clear to praise. The praise started with gratitude, gentle rumblings skirting over each other: the sun on our faces, healthy babies with gums shining, hope for the by and by, and then the tempo would rise, shouts would leap, and you couldn't catch one blessing, it was so mingled with the one before it: full bellies some of the time, and someone's mother died but she didn't suffer, and a man who's staying and a woman who said yes, and white folks being as good as they can be, and even if they showed themselves, who they really were, hope for the by and by, and Mama would stand up and start swinging her arms and switching her hips and slamming her feet down, and everyone surrounding her would follow suit. That was when the soil was fertile, that was when our minds could grow crops. Mama would remind us of all the stories we had heard about the women before us, many of whom made it rain without a cloud in the sky. Some of our fathers' men only had to point a finger for corn to grow. That's not what we were after, but then again it was too. My mama carved eighteen stones and only one of them had a star on it, and come summer, whoever picked that star would flee. It was our jobs to see they made it over.

Even now I can recall the little girl I was, pressing my mind into itself as hard as I could. The crisper the picture, the more likely the vision was to take place, Mama said, so I scrunched up my eyes and felt myself cushioned between my mother and father. I didn't know what North looked like, only that we were twenty miles west of New Orleans, but I imagined there was sunshine, a big fiery ball of it set low in the sky, and even as it was twisting up higher, I could almost touch it because I was running.

JOSEPHINE

1924

I am handing out hog head cheese sandwiches to the workers when I run into Major in the fields. He grips my arm as I pass him. I look away. I guess I'm still mad about the way he left me the other night, took Jericho with him. I know it's wrong, boy got a right to build his own life, but I can't outrun my hurt.

"You ain't gon' ignore me, are you, Mama?"

"Not ignoring you, just busy." A bit of the meat grazes my arm and I pick it off, flick it into the ground.

"And not just busy but mad," he adds, smiling his daddy's smile.

I don't say a word.

"Jericho has a function at the school tonight, you didn't forget, did you?"

I'm afraid I did.

"Eliza gon' make food for it, he gon' read

140

a speech. Eliza's people will be there too. It will be a nice time."

"One big happy family." I am looking down at my shoes.

He sighs. "That's what we are, ain't it? At least that's what I pray we'll be."

I spend the rest of the day ruminating on how the evening will go. Probably they're going to team up against me regarding ol' Aristide, convince me to pay him rather than cut our own yield short. I go over all the ways I'm going to counter, but my tongue is heavy the more I think about it, knowing I won't just be arguing against Major, that his new family will be there, and they can spin their words around me.

Naturally I pick up Link before I go. She is just sitting out on the porch, rocking, one foot hitched up on a box crate. She offers me a cool glass of water, and I shake my head.

"I was going to head over to see about Jericho then," I say.

"You? Was a time you said you wouldn't step foot in Eliza's house alive. Haunting, you said you would do."

"Oh, hush up. I never said anything like that. Anyway, the function's at the school, not their house. You got the legs to join me?"

"If you do, sister."

And we are on the path. The day's work is not done and we pass men in overalls and work boots, tugging corn stalks from the ears. A woman not much younger than me leans down over a sack of field peas, lifts a heavy board and thrashes it. Later, when there's wind, she'll drop the peas onto a quilt while their shells drift elsewhere. Now, the heat is steady, and I'm regretting not taking Link up on that glass of water.

I am more and more nervous the closer I get to the school. Link is right. It is Major and Eliza's show now. All this while, I didn't want to see them, but maybe I was afraid Eliza was the one who wouldn't want me. Not to mention her people are there, and whatever she is bringing to the table they're going to stand behind, holding it steady. Any time I have to work up a nerve, I close my eyes and imagine the Revisioners, standing in a row behind me, and I feel rooted, but it is hard to maintain that feeling here, now. I have to call up the visions of them more than once, and I find the edges of their faces are blurred.

The school isn't much, two small rooms in the back of the church that house children ages five to ten; battered books and chairs for every other child, a blackboard, a basket of switches and slates the children will hold in their laps. We can't complain though. The school a town over has windows that don't shut. They ran out of fuel halfway through winter, and the children sat inside wearing wool coats, their hands curled inside their pockets in tight fists.

Tonight, there is a wood platform set up outside the church for the children, and chairs lined up facing it for the audience to behold. The little girls sit on one side of a long log bench, and the boys on another. The program hasn't started by the time we arrive, and Jericho jerks out of his seat to wave at me and Link. He starts to step down to greet us but I hold my hand up to stop him. Eliza's people turn back to see who's riled him up so, and Link and I nod and move toward the row behind them.

The teacher introduces the program, calling for more students no matter if it's harvest season, and then it's the minister's turn to bless the event: "Oh Lord, cover the tongues of your tiniest servants, steady their hearts, and keep their minds straight." Jericho is near the back of his line, and a dozen children speak before it is his turn. The sun is setting in the distance, and the temperature cools enough for a shawl which I wrap around me. With the cotton on my skin, and the humming of little voices circling, it is impossible to stay alert. Several times Link has to kick my foot, and once Cyrile locks her eyes with mine just as my head nods back from a half dream. Finally, Jericho rises with his Bible in his right hand, and I sit up fast in my seat.

He reaches the center of the podium, opens up to a place he has marked, and his voice pokes out like a turtle's head out of a shell.

Wives, submit yourselves unto your own husbands, as unto the Lord. For the husband is the head of the wife, even as Christ is the head of the church: and he is the saviour of the body. Therefore as the church is subject unto Christ, so let the wives be to their own husbands in every thing.

The wonder of it still doesn't escape me, him reading like it's as natural as lifting his own head, or growing teeth.

Husbands, love your wives, even as Christ also loved the church, and gave himself for it; That he might sanctify and cleanse it with the washing of water by the word, That he might present it to himself a glorious church, not having spot, or wrinkle, or any such thing; but that it should be holy and without blemish.

He doesn't stumble over a single word, and when he's done, we all leap to our feet. Only a couple more boys read after him and I am fueled enough by Jericho's performance to pay attention. When it's over, Cyrile stands and turns back to greet us. She's wearing a wool suit with a flower pin securing the jacket; pearls reach her waist, and her hair beneath her wide-brimmed hat is wound in a sleek and plump bun at her neck. Louis seems to stand crooked though he's looking straight ahead at me.

I pat myself down on instinct. I should have worn better than this colorless dress I sewed from cotton sacks. I don't say a word, but Louis talks like he's responding to my thought.

"Nonsense, you look lovely." Then he draws me in and kisses me once on each cheek. He does the same to Link and I can see her trying to stop herself from laughing.

"Good to see you again, Miss Josephine," Cyrile says, hugging me fast.

Eliza and Major walk Jericho over from the platform, and Jericho nearly leaps into my arms.

"Mama, I was wondering when you were going to show your face," Major says. He points to the food in the back. The dishes the families brought are covered in towels on a long table behind us, and as long as the program dragged, much of it is probably still warm. "Eliza made cabbage and pork chops," he says.

"Now, it ain't your cabbage and pork chops," Eliza interrupts.

"It sure ain't," Jericho busts out laughing, then stops short when Cyrile cuts her eyes at him.

"Well, all that ham hock and fatback isn't so good for us anymore, now is it?" Cyrile says.

"You wouldn't know it from the flavor," I say, and Link and I are the only ones who smile.

After we serve ourselves, we walk back to our chairs, Link on one side of me, Major and Jericho on the other. Eliza and her people sit in the row ahead of us but they turn their chairs so they're facing us, partway. Louis blesses the food, and then we start in, Link stringing along the conversation with gossip.

"Come to find out those Shelton boys were scrapping over by the creek yesterday evening," she says. "Banged up the youngest one so bad he had to be taken to the hospital. Sat and sat waiting for somebody to treat him and by the time they called his name he said the bruise had gone from black to purple to just right brown again."

We all laugh, Eliza and her people less so.

"Yes, but the worst news came from old Marty Johnson," Link goes on. "I guess old Desiree collapsed one day right where she was dusting in the choir stand. Deacon found her when he went in for prayer worship Monday morning but it was too late."

"Oh." I put my fork down, but Link keeps eating, shoveling the cabbage and rice between her lips. "I'm sorry to hear that," I say.

"Yes, but that's not the end of it. I guess old Marty still heard her in the house even a week after the burial. They asked Willow to look into why she was haunting him, and come to find out, he paid another woman to lay with him the — afternoon — of — the — repast." She spaces that last part out. "Can you believe the gumption?"

I see Eliza and she just about looks like her stomach is turning so I say, "All right now, Link."

Link keeps right on though, "And not just once, but —"

So I repeat, "All right now, Link." And I

kick her foot, and she looks up with a jump and then clears her throat and turns back to her plate, and there's silence again, and I don't have to say it's not on account of the taste of the food.

"This is the first time we've all been together since the wedding," Eliza says in that squeak she uses.

The mother nods, cuts her meat with a fork and knife. I'm too old to learn to eat it that way and I pick the meat up with my fork and lean down and we meet in the middle. I like to think I still look like a lady.

"I'd like us to do this more," Eliza goes on. "Maybe once a season. I know it's a long way for you, Mama, and Louis, but we are family now, and soon we'll have a little one."

"Yes, indeed," I say when I'm done chewing. Louis sits on the other side of me. He has a big appetite and the rest of us aren't even halfway done when he walks back over to the table for more potatoes, more pork. When he's back, he gulps his lemonade before he zeroes in on Major.

"Now, how's the farm, brother?" he asks.

Major sits across from him, diagonally, and Louis looks him up and down. He is younger than Major, and it shows in their demeanors, but the way Louis talks to him now, you would think he was Major's daddy.

148

I can see Major getting nervous, chewing his food real firm, then clearing his throat more to collect himself than because there's something in it.

"It's good, brother," he says, looking him in the eye the way his daddy taught him. "Real good. In fact, I got some good news today. Ol' Aristide Taylor knocked on my door this morning and apologized. A few days ago, he started up a ruckus, thought he had a claim to some of my crop, but he turned around and said forget about it, I was right. He said I was right, Mama." He turns to me.

Eliza's steadily nodding.

I am surprised to hear that at first, but then it hits me. It's because I offered his son a job. A part of me wants to say that, but I don't want to embarrass my son. I won't have this family looking down on him any more than they might already do.

"This pork chop sure is tender," I lie.

"Best pork chop I ever had from you, Eliza," Louis repeats, plucking meat from between his teeth with a pick. It seems like we're on solid ground. There is a discussion of pound cake, though I'm not hopeful about it on account of the pork. Still I am feeling more and more comfortable there, when Link cuts in.

"You know why Aristide said forget about that cotton, right?"

Oh, Lord, she can't leave well enough alone. I move to kick her again, but I hit Cyrile instead and she jumps up startled.

"That's cause Josephine gave his son a job," Link goes on.

Major looks at me with a tired expression on his face, and I see the boy waiting on the front steps for somebody to come by and ask him to play, but not many kids ever did.

"Is that true, Mama? You gave him a job without talking to me?" he asks in a quiet voice.

"Since when the tail got to ask the head?" I say, trying to make a joke of it.

"Since you told me I could run the farm," he says, his voice louder.

"At the least you could have told us," Eliza says.

And I ignore her. She does best to let me ignore her.

Cyrile gets up and starts collecting the plates.

"Your daddy would be twisting in his grave if he knew you were objecting to me giving a man just back from the gang a means to make an honest living," I say, trying to maintain my composure.

"There you go," he says, "telling me what

my daddy would do. I knew him too, you know. He wasn't all yours, and I got him in me, in my blood. I see him every night before I go to bed, and he's telling me, don't do things the way he did them. He's telling me maybe that's why he didn't get where I'm trying to go."

I was softening at him saying he sees him nights, but now I stand. "Your daddy went from being a slave to owning three hundred acres, boy."

"And I'm trying to own four." He stands now, Eliza's hand in his.

I can sense the other families turning to look and I know this conversation will be retold many times come morning. Still I can't stop myself.

"I'm not going to watch you bury your daddy's legacy for a few dollars," I say. Link is up too now, next to me, leaning against the table for support.

Cyrile walks back with the cake, icing dripping down its sides, and I can look at it and see it's too dry.

"Everybody, shut up," she is trying to whisper but she isn't accustomed to scenes. "I told you not to bring up business matters at the dinner table," she turns to her son. "Now here you go again, making trouble."

Louis apologizes, but he is smiling in his

151

eyes. He helps me back into my chair.

Major and Eliza sit too while Cyrile slices the cake and dishes it out. I feel like I'm going to cry, but no. I won't allow it, so I take bites that fill the entire fork and I home in on the sweetness. I am done before I know it, and despite Cyrile's complaints, I get up and help her wash the dishes off with the pail of water beside the platform, then load them back into the basket. I walk back to the table just in time to hear Louis trail off.

"First thing you gotta do," he says, patting Major on the back, "is stop talking to women about men's business."

Major laughs from deep down in his belly. When it's time to go, I barely look at him I'm so disappointed. Cyrile squeezes me to her as if to make up for the quick pats I get from my own child. I walk a few steps in the direction of home, then turn back. The school is still in rock-throwing distance. I suppose I want to catch Major's eye, to give him a chance to meet my own, but he is lost in his conversation with Louis, and the sight of him so removed from me takes my breath away.

JOSEPHINE

1855

"A new man," I said to Missus the morning Jupiter arrived.

"A new slave," she corrected me from behind. She was a tall, fair woman with a red face and long blond hair that she scarcely combed, that she'd wash, sometimes, and just let hang. She was prone to having fits and she laughed like a wild animal screeching. You could always hear her rooms away heeing and hawing in high-pitched yelps. Mama called her a silly woman because she wasn't in control of her feelings. When they rose to their feet, she bowed in submission, where Mama handled hers like stew on a low fire.

"A rascally looking slave too," Missus added, and I agreed with her even though she was wrong. I could already sense Jupiter's power. It wasn't just his height, which was magnificent, or his color, the deepest shade of black I'd seen. No, he walked like his steps were measured, like God had already whispered to him how many breaths he was allotted this life, and he was well within his limit.

Ten years at Wildwood, and I only remembered one funeral. There must have been dozens more. Babies died before they were born, women died carrying them, men died on the fields, children coughed one morning and were out the next. But it was only this one, a woman who fell out when she was cooking pork for jambalaya, that stuck with me. She had been standing in the kitchen, stirring a pot with no known ailment in the world, when she hit the floor. Mama said not three minutes later, a baby was born in a cabin less than ten yards away to let them all know the woman's soul had found freedom.

Still at the burial we all cried, even my mama, who led the night procession from the quarters to the grave lit by pine-knot torches, singing all the while.

I've been praying this prayer a long time
I've been praying this prayer a long time
I've been praying this prayer a long time
And I ain't got weary yet

When the ceremony was over, we walked the mile back to the cabins, past the mule trough and the overseer's house, the saddle shed and the barn, the sugar fields and the brick mill where, before winter, children loaded the carrier with cane. Jupiter was standing outside our door, barefoot in a browned linen shirt and dusty trousers. The plantation was full of pigeons that flew through the fields for worms and grain but a single one stood next to Jupiter's right foot. This one barely had a beak, which made its icy grey head look like a round, worn stone. The bird wasn't poking at the dirt or fluttering its wings; it stood, head high, chest out, like a man. Mama didn't bat an eye at the man or the bird but let Jupiter in like she'd been waiting for him. She told me to shush and she boiled berries for tea in a pot on the fireplace. There was a pallet of dried grass in the center of the room, and without her telling me to, I walked over to it and sat, stretching the range of my ears so I could hear them. Mama had a large nose that flared at the nostrils and waiting eyes that could land on whomever she was beholding and just sit. She rested those eyes on him now. She asked what he wanted from her, and he said it was her doing the wanting. She said there wasn't anything she ever wanted from a man in all her life, and I felt betrayed on behalf of my daddy who had surely deserved desire.

There were twins three cabins down, and watching them was like watching those two. There was a conversation going on beneath the one I was observing, and I could understand that it was happening, but I couldn't make out the meaning.

Then he walked up behind her and started kneading the dough she held, though I had never seen a man put his hand in Mama's food. I saw that their hands were almost the same color. I had come out somewhere in the middle of Mama and Daddy, who was nearly white on account of his father being Tom.

Jupiter said my mother's grandmother sent him. Then he started to hum a song I had never heard before. Mama's eyes widened and she held on to the side of the round table where she worked. She said her grandmother had been dead more than twenty years; she said nobody knew that song but her and her mama, but her words came out on a slant.

He paused for a while, and even when he spoke, he didn't answer her. "I know what you're doing down there by the swamps. I ain't the only one who knows. Not the only one who wants to join either."

Mama's head hung in her hands, her proud heavy hair that she braided at night with oil. I wanted to tell her what it was she always told me: don't let anybody cause you to look down. On the outside for the white folks, sure, but inside where only you can see, be lording above them, be higher than they can set their minds to.

She shook her head again. There were rules, she said, and there wasn't no way people were going back on them. She wouldn't let them even if they wanted to.

He gripped her wrist, lowered his voice, but I could still hear him. "Every rule got a way inside it," he said, "a way to twist it around."

Mama shook her head again. "Not these rules," she said; "these rules too special, too important. If people started misremembering these rules, they'd get a mind to misremember others. The only thing standing between me and a whooped hide is these rules," she repeated.

If Daddy were here, he would have talked some sense into them both, would have said it would be worse than a whipped hide if they were caught. I knew because I listened to him talk to Mama, just the way I was

157

listening to Mama and this new man now. I'd heard Mama remind Daddy that Master let them call him Tom. "He's lenient about other things too," I'd heard her say. But Daddy would always snap back in a final word, "I know that man better than anyone on account of his blood running inside me, and some days I wake up mad enough to kill. That's from him, that's from his blood-line, and I'm telling you as sure as I can say my own name, Tom or no Tom, he got the power and the inclination to snap your neck."

The door opened. I could see the leather tops of Daddy's shoes before I saw him. He worked in the house, stood behind Tom while Vera served food. It was Carnival season and after a bite to eat, he would go right back to the big house to gather Tom and his brother and drive them down the levee road to the King's Ball. Because of that, even with the heat bracing for sum-mer, Daddy still wore his white gloves and his fancy vest, his livery coat trimmed with wool and lace. Watching him stand next to Jupiter and Mama I was ashamed of how white he was, how nearly straight his shoulder-length hair lay. He fought against his coloring his whole life, and the way he walked in the cabin that day like it maybe

158

wasn't even his home, I wondered if he picked Mama because she was the blackest woman on the plantation. He set his burlap sack on the table.

"Who is you?" he asked the man, though I knew he knew. He had to know.

"I'm Jupiter."

"And I'm Domingo." Daddy lifted me as he said it. I wanted to turn his head away from them. As strong as he'd always been, I felt he needed protecting.

"I carved a new doll, Daddy," I said. He smiled at me but he stared in their direction. He didn't talk for a long time, then he sat down, plopped me on his lap, and drummed his fingertips against the table.

"What you want here?" he asked finally.

"Just passing through, we got people in the same place, that's all."

"He got people where my mama from," my mama said at the same time.

The man backed up toward the door. I felt triumphant watching him skitter off like a mosquito that had gotten shooed.

"It's nice when you run into home country people. Ain't that right, Winnie?" the man asked from outside. I saw that same pigeon was waiting on the other side of the door.

And Mama nodded, but she was back to kneading the dough, reaching for a skillet from the rack above her head, and we were back to our lives, I thought.

The next week, the Missus was in rare form. Tom's mother was coming but the visit didn't comfort her, it frightened her, so much you'd hear her shrieking out orders from the moment she woke up, floating from room to room pointing at imaginary stains on the baseboards or spots on the sheets. There were wide halls in the center of the house and rooms on each side of them, and each one had to be dusted. The floors were hardwood and had to be polished until they shined.

"She looks down on me 'cause I've only had one child," she cried out while we worked.

"One is plenty. Children ain't no form of competition," my mother assured her, but she went on like my mother hadn't said a word at all.

"She had ten of 'em and it shows, but she wants me to be like her, broad-hipped and flat-bosomed. Have you seen her with her shirt off, the way that one breast just hangs?"

Hours later Mama still sat beside the missus, rubbing her slicked-back hair, massaging her shoulders while she wept.

"Maybe if my husband was around, things would be different. It's not your husband's mama anymore. I spent so much time worrying about her and he left her just like he did me, wouldn't even see her when she died." Mentioning my grandmother, whom I never met, sent the missus into a fury, and she worked herself into a fit, chest heaving and wails erupting until she fell asleep, snot dripping into her mouth. Mama still had to sweep the floors from dinner and wash and dry the plates and silverware. I offered to help but she shooed me away.

"This not child work," she said, even though I could tell she was what she called bone-tired. "Sit down somewhere while you can," she said. "Sit down somewhere for me."

It was many hours past nightfall when she finished and we were only a few feet from our quarters when we heard the sound. The faint outline of a song if I listened. Mama had been so tired before we left the big house, but now, she seemed to fill up with energy. I didn't know where her new power came from: the grass swaying, the moon shining, but she gripped my hand in hers and she ran.

Everybody was already in a circle when we reached the swamps, and Mama took

161

her place in the center and started like she'd been there all along:

> We believe in one God
> Who is the Spirit of Life inside us
> We believe in the Soul that outlives
> The body and links us
> To all that came and all that follow
> We believe in the fulfillment of our destiny
> Through a cause beyond our imagination
> We believe that destiny is winding its way
>   back to us
> Even now

Then people threw in their woes. Earl said his knee was aching. Jessie said he was tired. Luther just lost his wife and he cried at the same time every day on the fields, while other men filled his bags. When it was Fred's turn, he was quiet. Mama ignored it for a little while, then I caught her glance at Daddy, and she started.

"What's this, Fred? What's wrong with you?"

He shook his head.

"Naw, what is it? Best a say it now so it don't grow too heavy, liable to get so it's too heavy for you to carry it by yourself."

He shook his head again but it was obvious Mama had started to twist whatever

162

knot was inside him loose.

"Just say it, Fred." This from my daddy.

Fred opened up his mouth, then closed it. Then he opened it again. "To hear the people tell it," he said in a cool, soft voice, "you ain't planning to draw this cycle."

Mama laughed but her mouth didn't move; the sound seemed to slip through the crack of her lips. "How you suppose I'm not drawing? Why you suppose I'm here before the crack of dawn if I'm not drawing?"

"Last year by this time we had already made a plan." It was true. Last year was the first year Mama had allowed people to pick the stones. Daddy had chosen the one with the star, but Tom's brother had gotten sick, and Daddy had had to drive Tom to see him through it.

"I told you we had to wait longer this time 'cause of the trouble with the Travis plot."

She was talking about what happened a few months earlier. Fifty slaves schemed to set fire to their own plantation, but they were caught and arrested just a week before it was set to burn. Every last one of them was hung. Then their heads were speared on posts dotting the Mississippi River. I hadn't seen it, but I'd heard people whisper that some of their eyes were closed, and

163

some of them weren't.

"Nobody's thinking about that anymore," Fred said.

"Any white person ever heard of it will be thinking about it for the rest of their lives, brother," Mama said.

Silence then. My mama was always doing that, inspiring silence.

Fred seemed to change course. "Well, even if we do draw, ain't no luck in it. I s'pose you just gon' pick yourself or your husband again."

Daddy wasn't but a person away from Fred, and he faked like he was going to strike him, and Fred flinched. The rest of the group laughed.

I could see Mama shaking her head. She didn't like discord; not just that, she forbade it. She said that's what white people wanted, for us to take ourselves down. We already did their work for them in the fields and in the house, and then so many of us did their work for them in our own minds.

"That ain't what this about," she said. "You know as well as I do don't nobody pick but God. You don't remember that, you might as well turn around and get out of here, 'cause you no good to us."

Fred didn't say anything after that. His brother walked up, stood between him and

my mama for some time, then without
warning, Fred leaned his head back and
belted out:

My Lord calls me
He calls me by the thunder
The trumpet sound within my soul
I ain't got long to stay here

And a quiet seemed to descend on us, a
quiet outside us and a quiet inside us too.
We all opened our mouths and joined him.

My Lord calls me
He calls me by the thunder
The trumpet sound within my soul
I ain't got long to stay here

It was like that the rest of the night.
Someone would shout out the words to
another song and the rest of the group
would pick it up like there was one mouth
moving for us all. I can't say how long we
worshiped there, but I know I fell asleep
and woke up again many times. Each time I
did, there was a different melody streaming
around me, a different prayer moving my
mama's lips. The last time I woke, my daddy
was carrying me, walking so light I couldn't
hear his feet fall on the grass. His heart was

beating fast against my cheek, but I wasn't scared.

It wasn't long before morning. That time, I woke up to talking. I assumed it was Mama and Daddy like always until I sat up and saw the back of Jupiter's head, the tight beads of knaps that stretched down his neck. He and my mama were sitting at the table like those twins I mentioned, like they grew up together sitting at a table just like this one, and it only took another piece of wood to bind them back together again. He had heard about Fred, he said, willy-nilly Fred. Even before last night, Fred had been going around telling everybody that last year was his year but ol' Domingo pulled and backed out. Mama didn't correct Jupiter or even look at him with scorn.

"Well, what do you think I should do then?" she asked. I had never heard my mama ask anybody for advice.

Jupiter started humming, a real low grunt in his throat, and her shoulders relaxed; she leaned back. It was that same song she said only her mama knew.

"See, you know how all of our people got a meaning?" he asked once he finished.

She nodded.

He said he had one too, that he was a wordsmith, that he could string words

166

together that you'd never think belonged, but when you heard them you'd say aha, they are part of the same family. "That's what you need me to do with Fred," he kept on. "Convince him he don't want to be a runaway, or maybe it's that y'all are doomed to fail anyway, or maybe it's that you plannin' on pickin' him, and he just needs patience, any one of those things I can have him believe as soundly as his own name. You let me draw and I'll do that for him and anybody else need mending, you watch."

"Boy, you better go on somewhere," Mama said.

But then he started humming again. To me it sounded like the dog that took sick some years past with a lump in his chest the size of my fist, but Missus wouldn't let us put him out of his misery. I tried to go into myself, envision that woman I could visit since I came back to life. I could see her more clearly than ever: she was a shade somewhere between me and my mama; she had a girl standing next to her who had to be her own daughter but her daughter was walking away from her, and I wanted to tell her to turn back, but that hum wouldn't let my words through.

I stood, walked right up to the table. They

both looked up, but my mama's eyes were hard on me, like she had been sleeping and I'd thrown a rock at her forehead to rouse her. It was harder on me than anything that had come before it, seeing that I was the burn and not the salve. But the humming stopped.

Ava

2017

I get a call in the middle of the night from an unknown number. I silence it but it rings again. It's a nurse from Ochsner. Am I Ava Jackson? My mother has been admitted. She was vomiting up blood, and the woman next door called the ambulance. I throw on clothes and hop in the car. My mother is on the eighth floor, and I try not to look in the other rooms as I search for hers, at the patients, their eyes closed and their mouths gaping.

"You could have called me," I say to her first thing, rubbing my hands together with the sanitizer I squirted on in the hallway. Even I know that the accusation is a shield against my sadness, my fear.

Her neighbor is right next to her in an armchair she's pulled up to the hospital bed. She stands when I walk in.

"You could have called me," I repeat.

169

"I didn't want to bother you over this little thing," my mother says.

"It's not little, Mama," I say back.

Her neighbor gestures for me to meet her in the hallway.

"I'm glad you were there, but she should have called me," I say as I walk out.

"She said you might be working," the neighbor says at the door. She pauses. "Anyway, can you stay for a while?"

"Of course," I say.

She seems like she's about to say something, but she goes back into the room for her purse instead, whispers something to my mother then walks out, toward the elevator. She turns back.

"She wasn't herself," she says finally. "When I got there, I stayed for a while because she wasn't herself. She was saying the right stuff, she looked all right, but there was something about her that seemed shook, like it was a different person in her body. That more than the blood is what scared me."

Later, the doctor comes in and explains that blood vessels in my mother's esophagus dilated and ruptured, that the gastroenterologist needs to band them to stop the bleeding. They escort us to the fourth floor for the procedure, my mother in a gurney. I wait in the lobby, then a few hours after she's taken, my mother is brought back out. I hold her hand all the way to the elevator and back up to the eighth floor.

"I'm here now, Mama," I say. "I'm here now, and I'm never going to leave you again."

Back in the room, I call Grandma's nurse to check on her sooner and text King to get a ride with one of the girls.

When my mother finally does wake up, I'm standing over her.

"Everything went great," I say.

It takes her a while to keep her eyes open long enough to respond.

She shakes her head.

"No," I say, "you're going to be just fine. They patched the vessels right up, and you're going to be just fine."

"I'm not worried about that," she says, shaking her head again. "That lady," she says.

"What lady?"

"I'm more worried about you," she says, and she spreads the sentence out, stopping after every two or three words, nodding off, then starting again. "And King," she goes on.

"I'm doing great, Mama," I say. "King is too."

"Hmph," she says. It seems like her eyes are watering. She turns to the side. "No, you're not either." She is facing the wall. "If you needed the money that bad, you could have just stayed with me," she says.

"No, Mama," I repeat what I always say. "I don't want to burden you. I don't want to lean on you. It's my time."

"It wouldn't have been a burden," she cuts me off. "You're my child. It wouldn't have been a burden, and it would have been better than what you got yourself into now. That lady —" she starts, then she nods off again.

"You got along so great," I say, but even as I hear myself say it, I know it isn't true.

"You always had issues with that side."

"What do you mean?"

She looks at me like she shouldn't have to spell it out. "You know what I mean. You don't really know your daddy. You were always trying to get him to pay attention to you."

"Yeah, but I'm over that now. I've been over that," I add.

"I got a bad feeling about that house," she goes on. "A real bad feeling, and you got King in there."

"It's just temporary, Mama," I say. "It's not so bad," I say again.

"It is." There are tears running down the side of her face now. "It is," she repeats.

The doctor comes in, and my mother tries to smile for him.

The surgery went well, he says. They'll continue to check her blood count. She can expect to get out in a few days as long as the hemoglobin levels keep rising.

"So who's the president?" he asks her.

"Barack Obama." I can tell she's joking. The doctor can too.

"Uh oh," he smiles. "We might have to open you up again."

"Then it's Michelle," she jokes.

She stops smiling as soon as we're alone again.

"I have something I want to ask you, but you can say no," she says. "I know you're busy."

"Anything," I say.

"My girls, I'm supposed to meet with them tomorrow; I would cancel but they're so close to delivery and they get nervous sometimes as the due date creeps up."

"That's fine, Mama, no problem," I say.

Then she closes her eyes again. I sit with her, thinking about what she said about the house, about Grandma Martha, for some time. When her neighbor comes back to relieve me, I lean over and kiss my mother.

She's muttering in her sleep with a pained expression on her face.

I rub her arm, and she quiets down, but she doesn't wake up.

My mother's girls want to meet at Hazel's house in the East. I cross the High Rise like I drove it yesterday though really I haven't been in this part of the city in years. I lived here briefly when I was a little girl, across the street from Resurrection of our Lord School. It was a booming suburb then, and everything we needed we could access off of Downman Road, Read and Crowder Boulevards, or Bullard Avenue. Every Friday, my mama and I would see movies at the Plaza. Saturdays, we made groceries at Schwegmann's then hit up Sam's for bulk food and samples. Weekend nights, we'd eat shrimp po'boys at Castnet or black-eyed peas at Causey's, and every Sunday after church, weather permitting, we devoured snowballs from Rodney's before we even left the parking lot.

But property values had plummeted even before Katrina ransacked what was left, and now at least half of those places were gone. Hazel lives in a redbrick house on a just-trimmed lawn with barred windows and doors. I park and walk up the driveway, ring the doorbell. She answers, bigger than when I saw her last, and happier. She welcomes me inside, where it's clean and simple: linoleum floors, two brown tweed sofas facing each other, and pictures along the walls. One is of Hazel pregnant, much further along than she is this time. She's notably younger in the picture too, and her hair is twisted in short dredlocks.

There are about twelve girls already here. Some are on the sofa just rubbing their bellies, looking ready to pop, and some of them are in the back eating. I can smell the food; if these girls are anything like my mama, it's from that vegan soul food spot she loves, and I'm not going to lie, their barbefu is what's up.

I hadn't told my mother but I was glad she asked me to come today. She'd been hounding me about working with her for years, and I'd resisted on principle, but the glimpses I'd had of her counseling those girls always spoke to me. It was something I knew I'd be good at, but it seemed too easy, like maybe then it wouldn't be worthwhile.

"Just calm them down," she'd told me on

the phone on the way over here. "You have a very calming presence. I don't know if you realize it. It's why Martha wants you."

And I didn't want to get into that again, so I hurried off the phone. Now Hazel gives me a quick tour of the rest of the house, her wide African-print skirt swirling, her basketball-shaped belly peeping out over her waistband. When we're back in the living room, she hugs me to her, a tight squeeze. She smells like Jergens lotion and incense.

"How is she?" she asks. "How's Gladys?"

I nod. "She'll be all right. They just need to monitor her for a few more days."

Hazel starts to tear up. "I was so worried when I found out," she says. "You know, she's like my mama too. The mama I never had. I'm just praying she gets out before the baby comes, you know. 'Cause I can't do it without her. I know I can't."

I don't know the girl, but my heart hurts for her.

"She will," I start. "But even if she doesn't," I say, "you got this."

"No, no, you don't understand. She's been counseling me. I have panic attacks, about what happened last time, and I just shut down. I can't do it without her."

I try to think of what my mother would

say. It comes to me, something like *It's a dif-ferent situation you're in now, baby.* Or maybe just *This child is going to live.* But I feel like a fake saying it that way.

"You have a name yet?" I ask instead.

The girl nods. "We picked out two, one for a girl, one for a boy."

"You ever say it?"

"Every day," she answers back.

"Good, good. And just imagine the baby," I say. "Imagine holding it in your arms. Watching it stare back at you, while you're saying that name."

She is tearing up again, but she nods. "I try to do all that, visualizing, but it just makes me sad sometimes, to think about the good stuff."

"That's all right, that's all right to feel sad. You're going to feel sad." I reach out and rub her arm.

She starts to cry more. "Miles," she says, "for the boy. That was my grandfather's name, Miles. And then Ella for a girl."

"That's real nice," I say. "Those are both real nice."

She looks up at me, then looks down again. "You look just like her. You lucky," she says, an accusation more than a compli-ment. "If Gladys was my mama, I'd just sit on her lap all day, have her feed me chicken soup. You ever do that?" she asks. She smiles. She has a gap between her front teeth. She is a pretty girl, brown skinned, and if the circumstances were different, I'd want to introduce her to King in a few years.

"She does make good soup," I say, and we laugh. Another girl approaches, and I break away from Hazel and make my rounds. I ask to touch everyone's bellies, feel the babies squirming under my hand. I toss compliments to them, catch them right back: they love my wedges, and I love how fly they make pregnancy look.

"When I was carrying King," I say, "we wore muumuus and sat down somewhere. Y'all look like you could be walking down somebody's runway."

Then Hazel lowers the volume on the music, and everybody sits, the most pregnant girls on the sofa and the smaller ones at their feet. I'm still standing in the front of the room, I see now, and I make my way down.

"Gladys likes to start off with a chant," Hazel says. She is sitting with the other girls, but closest to me. "I can start it," she goes on. She closes her eyes and opens her mouth. I recognize the sound. It is the same one I woke up to some mornings as my mother entered meditation, a cross between an *oh* and a *you.* Hazel's voice rises and falls, then more voices join the chorus. At first I wonder how long they can go on. I didn't sleep well the night before — on account of my mother's premonitions — and I feel like dozing. After a while, though, I start to sway; I even catch myself mouthing the chant. I'm a step removed from the real world when without warning the girls stop.

I don't want to open my eyes, and when I do, I find I'm a little loopy. The girls take turns talking about their week: some wonder if they dropped; one saw heavy discharge in her panties and thought it was amniotic fluid leaking. She went to the doctor and they monitored her for four hours and sent her home; she was just paranoid she guessed.

"Better safe than sorry," I say.

The girls echo that sentiment.

"I'm scared though, more and more," Hazel says. "I have a little while, but my dude is acting all funny, doesn't want to commit to moving in like he said he would, but I got all the stuff, the car seat, the crib. All that's at my house, so if he wants to see the baby . . ." she trails off. "I just hate that he's ruining it for me," she says. "This is supposed to be the happiest time of my life."

And I understand. The month after I had

180

King, I was thrilled to have a baby but the baby seemed to bring out the worst in his father. All of a sudden the man couldn't stay home. I thought at first it was the women, but one day I looked out my front window, and he was just sitting in his car. He had been out there for hours. I don't think about it anymore but being in front of this room brings it back.

"It can be both," I say. "Both happy and sad. I mean, we're not living in a fairy tale. For us, it's got to be both. Like for me, it didn't take long before I realized my husband and I weren't going to be able to make it, and I was angry about it, believe me. That wasn't how I expected my life to look. But then I had this baby that my husband and I had created, and I couldn't stop looking at him, and caring for him gave me a peace I hadn't even known existed. At the end of the day, that canceled it out, all the self-pity. I didn't feel like I had the right to complain about a thing, you know. God didn't owe me a thing if he gave me the baby in my arms."

Hazel leads another chant before we disperse.

I stay for a little while after that. The barbefu is bomb just like I expected, and the girls turn on music and are surprised that

181

at my age I know who Cardi B is, and not only that, but that I can rap along to every word of "Bodak Yellow."

On the drive home, I remember that time again just after King was born. I hadn't said this to the girls but it was my grandmother who saved me. She folded onesies and sat with the baby, yes, but she also got me up and she shook me real hard, and she said, "That baby over there," and she pointed at him. She said, "He needs you, okay, he needs you."

Even when I disagreed, she went on.

"He's your child," she said. "He's yours, not anybody else's. You're the only one who can take care of him the way he needs to be taken care of. I can't do it. His daddy can't do it; it has to be you. He deserves you, and you deserve him."

I'd tapped that first month down, forgotten that Grandma Martha was the one to lift me. I suppose I could have turned to my mother, but she hadn't become Yemaya yet, and I didn't know if I could trust her not to see me as pathetic. And I don't know what's going on with Grandma now: the strange clothes, the unkempt appearance, the outbursts. Of course it has crossed my mind that it could be dementia, but I'm rooting for it to be anything else, stress, dehydration, something she can come out on top of. Either way, there's no question she's not one hundred percent, and I owe it to her to see her through.

When I get to the house, King is already asleep. The nurse says it's been a rough night. Grandma was out of sorts most of the day looking for me.

I'm prepared for the worst going up the stairs, but she is smiling when I walk in. I tell her about Hazel and the girls and how well the visit went, but then the reason I was there instead of my mother stirs the grief that's been building. I sit on her bed and let it all out.

"She's fine now, but it could have gone the other way," I say. "As much as we've been through, my mama's the only person in this world who's always there for me. And if she's not here, I don't have nobody."

"You have me," she says. "I know she's going to be fine; she's a tough lady, but you have me too." She pulls me into her for an embrace. "I'll be saying a prayer for her tonight," she says as she rubs my back, and she shifts in the bed to reach over for her rosary.

Sure enough I hear her chanting as I walk back to my own room:

183

I believe in God, the Father almighty,
   creator of heaven and earth, and in
   Jesus Christ,
His only Son, our Lord, who was
   conceived by the Holy Spirit.

JOSEPHINE

1924

After Jericho's performance, I drop Link off, go home, and take a hot bath. My fight with Eliza and Major is still weighing on me though, even after I settle under the sheets. I have trouble sleeping that night. The next morning it takes me a long time to get out of bed. Finally, I only rise and dress because I know Charlotte is coming, and I don't want her to see me in my bedclothes. Sure enough, she is at my door after lunch.

"This is beginning to be a habit," I say to her, like it is unwelcome. The truth is, though, for that morning it had been what got me standing.

"I hope it's no bother," she says, already at my table. She has another jar of jam with her, and she hands it to me like it is the visitation fee. "I know you have things to do and family to care for and everything else, but I don't have nobody here. It's just me and Vern. And he's gone half the time, and as lonely as it gets, at least it's better than — than sitting there with him. My mama said she could tell a lot by a man's shoes, but I don't think that's true. I don't think you can tell much at all."

She looks up then, and I catch the mark around her eye.

Oh, so he is that sort of man. My own had been the opposite, a saint when he could have been vengeful, loving when resentment was right at hand. But I have seen this sort my whole life, mostly in visions while women sat across from me, begging me to give them something that might make him stop. But there was nothing to give. I told them that, time and time again. Still they didn't heed me and some had lost their lives. I make the sign of the cross.

"Lord, deliver me," I say. "What's happened to you?"

"Oh, this? Well, it's nothing."

"It sure don't look like nothing to me, girl."

"Well, he gets so angry sometimes. See, he's just starting out, and the crops aren't thriving, and then everything with the baby. I can't seem to grow one, and when I do, I can't keep them."

"Might be on account of that."

186

"No, he never does it when I'm carrying." She shakes her head. She is stubborn about this one thing, gripping it to her.

"Yeah, but the stress."

She looks up then. "It'll be different once the crops start coming in," she says. "If you think of it, say a prayer for me on that. Or the baby. Matter of fact, pray for the baby first, if you get to it, 'cause I think if the baby's here, he won't mind as much what else is going on. All this while he just thought we'd have a little one in our arms, or one on the way, and I haven't even let him carry the hope, so he's sad, and it comes out like anger. And my mama said you could tell a lot about a man by his shoes, but if she'd come visit me, I'd tell her that's not true. My mama makes a lot of bad decisions in her life, and in a lot of ways I had to raise her, but this time I would tell her, that's not true. So in case there's a man in her life she needs to judge, she'll know to find another way."

I am only newly awake, and it is a lot to wake up to, and I don't speak. Sometimes people want me to say something, to offer up a word that might smooth the matter over, cover it, but it is the silence that illuminates the peace. All of a sudden it is important to me that this child has some peace.

"Where does your mama live?" I ask.

"Forty miles east."

"That's not so far."

"Far without a carriage or a horse."

I nod. "That's right."

"But Vern doesn't abide trips of that nature. If I go, he wants to come with me, and he doesn't have the time. So she'll have to come here. I tell her that, but . . ." she trails off.

I get up to refill her coffee. People tell me all manner of things, stories you wouldn't believe if I repeated them, and I am careful to separate myself from their woes. I have to be.

"Sometimes I think it's God," she says. "After all this, the way my life has turned out, I don't know if I can count on him; I don't know what to believe, but sometimes I think he's protecting me. A baby doesn't deserve to be born into this mess."

"No," I say.

"Yeah, so maybe don't pray on it," she says. "Maybe pray that I stay as barren as I've ever been. Maybe pray for me to get up the courage to leave one day; maybe that's what God wants for me, and without a baby maybe that will be easier."

I am looking out the window now. If I look at her, some of that sadness will pass through because I wasn't expecting this, I hadn't steeled myself for it. If she asks about the baby now, how to grow one inside her, I might cover my altar with blue cloth, a jar of molasses, and a glass bowl of water. I might tell Charlotte to finger each of my mother's old stones, then clean them, line them in a circle around the water.

I probably wouldn't; it messes a child up to see his mama hit, plus I've long forsaken magic. But I might.

As for now, I pass her a cup of coffee with my eyes on the table, and she doesn't finish it. She stands up after a while and says she has to fix Vern his supper, and she is out the door before I can say *Take that jam back with you. I couldn't eat it all if I tried.*

Later Link, Theron, and Jericho come over for dinner and a game of whist. I am still troubled by what I saw earlier, but having them there with me is the greatest contradiction. There aren't people in the world I feel more comfortable with, and the only thing greater that I can imagine is closing my eyes and seeing my mama welcome me to the sweet beyond. Link brought a coffee cake she sliced and hands out plates at the table. I push the one she passes me back, ask her if she's saving the bigger slices for her better friends.

"Do you want a slice or a hunk?" she asks, and we all laugh.

It is silent while we eat at first, aside from the occasional moan. There is the sugar and the butter and the cinnamon to observe and a splash of vanilla makes all the difference, then —

"Who was that white woman by your house the other day?" Link asks. "I was walking by and I saw her coming out. Plain-looking mousy old thing. Her husband got a few cows but she don't have the sense to put their milk in her own belly."

We laugh again.

"Well, she's been coming over a bit," I say.

They look up from their food at that, a mix of concern and shock wrinkling their faces.

"Coming by to do what?" Link asks. She has set her fork down.

"Just to talk, she's lonely." I already regret saying as much as I've said. There was no need to is all. "She can't have a baby," I add.

"I could prepare my bath with white women's tears," Link says.

"Not just yours but all of ours," Theron

adds. Jericho isn't thinking about us, just that coffee cake. No, it isn't mine, and missing lemon rind, but there is no question it is second best, and in a few years she might surpass me.

"Anyway she's becoming a friend."

Link drops her fork. "Now, sister, you don't want no part of that," Link says. "Not a half of a part, nor a quarter. Our people can't be friends with theirs, you know that. They're not capable of it. They think *friend* mean *mule.* They think *friend* means they can take and take and you never get tired of giving. Suppose you don't give her what she think she deserve," she goes on. "All that disappointment gon' turn to rage and all that rage gon' fall on you."

"I know, sister." I am embarrassed now. That I needed to be told that. "I wasn't asking for advice," I say. "I was just sharing my day with you, that's all."

"Oh," she quiets down. "Well, just so long as you know you don't want no part of that, sister. No part."

I nod, feeling very much like a child, and I am not a stranger to that feeling. As the years tick on I find I become smaller inside. "That's what I told her," I say. "I told her that in so many words already."

They all nod and grunt, back to their food.

I excuse myself for my bedroom. I splash clear water on my face from the bucket I filled that morning, stare into the mirror. Now, this I could do without. Over seventy years. Sunken eyes, sagging neck. It feels like my missus is staring back at me, black as I am and white as she was. Aside from Link, she was the only woman I had seen start growing old.

I walk back toward the kitchen. I can hear them talking about me from the hallway.

"You think she's all right?" Theron asks.

"She's fine, she's just being Josephine. She comes off as rough but it's the opposite, going and feeling compassion for people who would hang her out to dry if they got the chance."

Then Jericho chimes in, his little boy voice seeming out of place in that kitchen, in that conversation.

"She's partial to white girls. Maybe," he adds. "That neighbor probably reminds her of her little friend."

"What friend?" Link asks.

"The missus' daughter. When she was a slave. They were like sisters, then Mama Josephine ran away."

I clear my throat and walk back in all cool, though hearing Jericho sends those old feelings rushing back, that same sadness I'd felt leaving Miss Sally, guilt too, knowing my mama wouldn't have approved of befriending the mistress' daughter enough to miss her; maybe that wasn't the right way to say it. It wasn't that she wouldn't have approved, she wouldn't have thought it was possible.

It was the reason I had never mentioned Sally to Link.

"Oh, Jericho, you can't hold water. You sharing my old plantation secrets." I rub his head to let him know I'm not mad. "Those are just bedtime stories," I say.

But when my visitors are gone and I am done with the dishes, I pace the floor for hours, kneading my fist into my thigh, fighting the pictures popping up in my mind. Still they won't surrender.

JOSEPHINE

1855

Miss Sally was slow to develop, and her daddy thought by me being six months older she might mimic me as I grew. He forced us together. Her mother was against it, said there was nothing her daughter needed from a slave, but sure enough it wasn't long before my head only came to Miss Sally's chin, and she was teaching me my letters.

And I taught her how to create things that were not there. Started out with coins.

"Call those things which be not as though they were," I'd say.

"What in the grace of God does that mean?" she'd ask. She had blond hair that her mother let mat, and she was a skinny thing, on account of her baby sickness. But she didn't seem to know any of that. She'd get so excited sometimes and her joy would pass over to me in a way that I didn't know

194

was possible between blacks and whites.

And I'd think about her question and shrug. "I don't know." We'd fall into each other giggling, but when we'd settle down, I'd repeat it just the way Mama did.

"You see the dollar piece in your hand? Close your eyes until you see two of them so crisp at the edges you can feel the ridge when you reach for them."

She'd obey for a while, then she'd open her eyes.

"There's nothing there," she'd say. "Wait till I tell Papa. You're just as ordinary as the day is long. I'm just kidding, Josephine." She'd reach for my arm. "I would never do that to you. Even if you're no more special than a jar of milk, or than I am for that matter."

She'd squeeze me and I'd squeeze her back. Her mother would shriek down the stairs all, "Get your hands off my daughter, Josephine. You're getting too old for that now," and we'd spread apart like peas from chaff.

Then one night Miss Sally came to the cabin after dinner, and we sidled outside beneath the oak.

She was so excited she couldn't begin until finally I held her arms and forced her to look at me square in the face. I said her name real firm the way Mama talked to me when she was telling me something important about white folks. Finally Miss Sally started.

"Remember that dollar piece that we wanted to make two? This evening my daddy came back with my uncle from Georgia, and he asked me who was more handsome, him or my daddy, and he pulled a coin from behind his ear, and I said he was of course, and he gave it to me; don't you see, Josephine, don't you see, you created it; it is true what everybody says about you, you're powerful, you're magic, you're — you're special." She hugged me to her then, and I felt embarrassed.

"I didn't create anything," I said. "Your uncle's the one who created it."

"Don't be so modest," she said back. "Do you know what *modest* is?"

"No," I said, but I could have figured it out.

"It's when you don't think high enough of yourself. Jesus was modest. He died a prisoner's death to save us from our sins."

I nodded. "I know." The preacher said as much on Sundays, but Mama said no God of hers was saving white folks from a thing.

Miss Sally pulled the coin out of her pocket. "I want to give you this," she said.

"Oh no, Miss Sally, I couldn't take that." It was hers after all, and I could hear what Mama would say: *A white woman don't give without expecting something in return.*

But she insisted. "No, Josephine, I wouldn't have it without you. Now you take it now." She held my hand open and pushed it inside, then closed my fist.

"You won't tell anybody, will you?" I asked. I was thinking about her mother, who no doubt would say I stole. It'd be a lie, we'd all know it, but she'd grip it tight because she couldn't abide what the truth would mean.

"And give up my secret all-powerful magician?" Miss Sally laughed and pulled me closer to her. "Of course not. This is our secret. Not just because of the magic either." She whispered the next part: "I'd never do anything to hurt you, Josephine. You're like a sister to me."

Then a few weeks later, I was fanning her off from the heat. She had nothing but her petticoat on and was quieter than normal before she turned to me without warning.

"I wonder if you could create other things too, not just coins," she said.

"Like treasures?" I asked. "Jewels?"

"Maybe something other than that?" she asked. "Maybe a baby for Mama. She tries every year, but they keep dying. It has made her heart like stone."

Is that what it is? I thought, but didn't say.

"I guess I could try, Miss Sally. Does she want a boy or a girl?"

"I think by now she just wants a baby; any one will do." She paused. "But I heard her say once if she had another daughter she'd have to keep going because Papa wants a son."

I didn't tell her but I started right then, rocking the layers of my mind back and forth to the rhythm of the legs of a chair, and there was Missus inside it, her arms full. I drew a picture of a baby boy on a scrap of paper, folded it seven times, and added it to our altar that night. And I wanted it too. Mama said half of it is in the feeling tone, and I was wanting it for Missus, not because of her, a woman whose heart pumped vinegar through her veins, but because of Miss Sally, who had never seemed so somber since I'd known her.

"And, Josephine?" she asked like she already knew what was in my head. "When you're picturing it, can you picture me beside Mama, and maybe her hand is holding mine? And maybe she is saying I love you?"

■ ■ ■ ■

It didn't take but a month. Missus wasn't showing yet, but she was sick, and Miss Sally said she knew something was in there, she could just feel it.

"Daddy can feel it too," she said. "He's walking around here like the world is sitting on his right shoulder. He caught a slave in the bread bowl yesterday and didn't even flog him, that's how happy he is."

"What slave?" I asked.

"That new one. Jupiter. Daddy says he knew he wasn't nothing but trouble, that he shouldn't have taken him on. Uncle couldn't do nothing with him though, and Mama says Daddy can't say no to his brother, on account of Uncle's mental faculties being as soft as they are. Mama says we'll be carrying Uncle's burdens for the rest of our lives."

"So what, did he let him keep the bread?"

"Yeah. That's how I know there's a little baby in there, Mama ain't as big as two fists put together, but I can always tell by Daddy. He said by the time that boy was through with him he had spun him a tale clear from here to the other side of Georgia. He got to thinking maybe he was the one who took the bread his own self. He wasn't sure. He said that's one powerful slave, and Uncle just didn't know how to use him, that's all. But I don't think he is powerful at all. I think it's you who's powerful. And pretty soon we going to have a pretty little baby in our arms to show for it."

But it wasn't true that he wasn't powerful. Not true in the least. Because the next morning Missus walked out onto the porch holding her stomach. The porch wrapped around the house and sometimes she stood on it facing the river and sometimes, like today, she stood on it facing the fields. It seemed like her face changed depending on which way she was looking. Today it looked old and worn. She called all the slaves down, and I stood with my parents at the edge of the cane. It was the hardest time of the year, grinding season. There was only so much time to prepare the crop for harvest. Tom had delayed as much as possible so the cane would be sweet but that meant every field hand rose earlier than sunup, returned later than sundown; that they cut, loaded, and carried the cane for milling on Sunday even.

And Missus walked the plank of the porch back and forth, back and forth.

"I'm missing something," she said. "I'm

not going to say what it is, just that it's gone, and somebody out there knows where it is. The thing itself is very valuable to me. It's a family heirloom of sorts, and the idea of it being hauled off my property right in front of my very own eyes" — she touched her mouth like she was going to start to cry — "well, it's heartbreaking." All the while she talked, she kept walking.

"I'm going to stand out here with you until the first person confesses. No food or water neither, and for every hour you're out the field, that's a lash. But I'm going to find that" — she paused — "that heirloom. The truth is," she quieted, "it's not the heirloom as much as it is the trust. That's something that can't be repaired. Even when I get it back. My husband and I, we go out of our way to not treat you the way everybody else does, but maybe we've been naïve."

Tom stood in the doorway, in his trousers and silk stockings, smirking at the scene, and she glanced over at him.

"Maybe we've been naïve," she repeated. "We've certainly tried to give you the benefit of the doubt."

Just then Jupiter raised his hand and I could see the edge of a long, thick knife in his grip. People said he cut more cane than anybody, even men who had been doing it all their lives. I had seen him from the house myself, so tall he had to bend more than the others to clip the flags, then the green top, next the stalk at its root.

"Yes, are you confessing?" Missus seemed excited at the prospect.

He shook his head in wild swoops, that pigeon that followed him still at his feet. "No, ma'am, Missus, ma'am, I am not, just want to tell you I know what it is you lost. It couldn't have been me that's taken it 'cause I've been in the field, you have seen to that, but I just want to say I know what it is you lost, know where it is too."

She seemed disarmed, and she looked through him more than at him.

"It's your grandmother's earrings," he went on, and Missus's hand dropped to her side. "She didn't give them to you, your mama did, on your wedding day, told you they were real diamonds, and they're not real diamonds but you believed they was, 'cause your mama said it, and even when you found out the truth, it only made you love your grandmamma more."

"Where are they?" she asked in a soft voice.

"They fell behind the head of your bed, that's all. Nobody took them. Go upstairs, venture underneath, you'll see them. They sure do sparkle."

She went upstairs and came back down holding the not-diamonds in her hands, but she directed the overseer to beat Jupiter anyway, to drive three stakes in the ground, two at the top for each hand, and one at the bottom for both feet. The whole while he hung there, Missus whistled the tune of one of the songs I'd hear her sing Sundays on her way back from church, "Amazing Grace."

When it was all over, I walked with Mama home.

"I hate her," I said, slowing down, kicking my feet until the dust swirled at my knees.

She turned around, gripped me to her, and slapped my face. Then she knelt down beside me, and pulled me into her. I could feel her heart beating. We were so close together we could have been one. She backed up.

"Now, hate," she started, "ain't no use in hate, Josie. Ain't no use in hate," she repeated. "Whatever you trying to get away from, hate just binds you to it. You find, even when you think you found a way out, God will bring it back to you, slap you right in the face with it. Where you thought it had gone missing. So don't ever say *hate*."

"And especially don't say it so loud one of them can hear you." It was Jupiter. I turned to face him. He was shining, good as new, like it wasn't him tied to those stakes an hour earlier.

My mama seemed like she was holding herself back from embracing him the same way she'd just embraced me. She stood there beholding him for longer than was natural. Far longer.

"How you know about those diamonds?" she asked finally.

"I done told y'all they weren't diamonds," he said. But he didn't answer the question, he just repeated himself. "They weren't diamonds, that was the thing about them. Although the way they sparkled, I could see why she thought they was."

That night there was a banging on the door. Daddy was in the bed, holding on to Mama from behind. He didn't hear the knock, and it was Mama who stood up to answer.

"Winnie, come quick, Missus's bleeding out," Vera shouted from the other side.

Mama dashed for her sack and then sprinted off. I trailed behind her but no one saw me go.

We reached the house, then upstairs. Missus was moaning on the bed, and she reached for Winnie. "Not again," she said. "I can't do it again."

Mama nodded and pulled back the sheet. "I'm sorry, Missus," she said.

"I don't care about sorry," Missus said back, and she started to wail. I could see my mother's hands from where I stood. There was a pool of blood beneath Missus's bottom and Mama lifted her to set down quilts. Then Mama reached up Missus' pee hole. Missus gasped but Mama kept going. I wondered if Mama ever thought about squishing Missus' insides together, making her hurt. Mama held so much power in her fingertips.

"Everything feels normal, Missus," Mama said.

Missus was relieved but couldn't accept it. "But the blood," she said.

"It happens sometimes. Happened with Josephine," Mama said. She still didn't know I was in there.

"So everything's going to be okay?"

Mama nodded.

"You sure, Winnie?" Missus asked again between gasps.

"Certain," she said, and I wondered how Mama could be certain of something so grand. Then she turned for the door. On her way to the stairs she saw me, and called

205

me to her with her eyes, but she was not down one step before there was another gasp, this one louder. Then a scream, "Winnie," and Mama jerked back inside. There was more blood now, more than I had ever seen and I closed my eyes against it, imagined it halting, imagined the source of it all closing in on itself and imagined that rocking chair, tilting back and forth, back and forth, and there was a baby boy in it, Missus holding him, a bonnet. I ran the scene through my head like a wheel turning over and over and over again.

Mama was frantic. I could hear her panting, and Missus moaning, the sounds mingling so I could barely focus, but I fixed the picture in my mind. It didn't take long for things to slow: Missus stopped screaming, and Mama's hands were on me. I opened my eyes. Mama was pressing me toward the stairs. I looked back at Missus. It seemed her bleeding had stopped, but she stared at me like I had taken something from her, something final that would never be returned. As we walked down, I saw Tom at the foot of the steps waiting, gripping the rail so hard his knuckles were red, and he said, "You see to it she has that baby this time, Winnie," and Mama said, "By the grace of God," and Tom said, "I'm not talking about God, I'm talking about you, Winnie."

She smiled at him, but she was angry when we got outside.

"What were you doing when your eyes were closed like that?" she asked as we walked. The sun hadn't come up yet, and it was cold, colder than I'd known it could get in the open night air. The hair on my arms stood straight up like grass.

"Nothing," I said.

"Don't lie to me, Josephine. I know it wasn't nothing. What were you doing?"

I shook my head. "I didn't mean to cause any trouble," I said. My lower lip was trembling.

"You're going to cause trouble if you don't tell me. I need to know what you were doing in there."

She stopped just before we reached the cabins and knelt before me.

"I just saw the blood stop flowing," I said. I was crying. "I saw whatever was leaking closing up, I saw her holding a baby, rocking it. It's a boy."

"It is a boy." She said it like it was bad that it was a boy though, bad that the baby existed all around, and she gripped my hands and kept walking.

"How long have you been able to do that?"

"Not long."

"Have you ever done it before?"

I shook my head, deciding not to tell her about the coin. "Is it bad, Mama?" I asked. "If it's bad, I won't do it again."

She shook her head, patting the soiled apron on her dress with her hands. "It's not bad, it's good, it's the only good thing in this world, our power to step outside it. But I don't want you doing it again, not like that, not for them."

"Why not, Mama? If it's the only good thing?"

"It's the only good thing when we do it, for ourselves and for each other. But they take, they take, and they take, and pretty soon it's not yours anymore. It's not pure, and with the purity goes the power. Like me today, I was trying to make the bleeding stop too, you know." She lowered her voice then. "But it wouldn't take. I saw her in the chair, rocking and rocking. But it wouldn't take."

"I'm sorry, Mama," I said. "Why did it work for me? Did I take it from you?"

"No, baby girl, don't ever think that. They took it from me. They took it from me. And if they realize it's gone, they're going to toss me out with it. But I'm gonna get it back, I'm gonna take it with me, and I'm gonna get it back."

Then she looked away. I turned to where her line of vision led me. It was Jupiter, coming in from the swamps, mud streaming down his pant legs to his bare feet. His bird was just as covered, but it was in the air now, near Jupiter's shoulder, and when it flapped its wings, mud dropped onto the tip of Jupiter's ear.

"Where you coming from like that?" Mama asked.

"You didn't see me. I was right there with you."

Mama squinted at him.

"No?" he asks in disbelief. "No matter, I was there. A shame that bleeding stopped, don't you think?"

Mama gasped, stepped backward. "Don't you wish no harm on that baby. I won't lower myself to the point where I'd allow it."

"I didn't wish no harm on that baby. Why its heart's still beating. One of the reasons." He looked at me then.

Mama grabbed my wrist and turned off to the side toward the cabin.

He didn't follow her. When we got to the front door, she turned back. He was still talking like we'd never left.

"She should have been happy when I told

her where those earrings were," he started. "But she don't know the difference between weakness and strength; she scared off by power, even power that could ease her mind." He smiled again, looked at us like he was coming out of a daze. "Nah, the baby's okay," he went on. "For now. The thing about those diamonds," he said, "is they not even real." Then he stretched out his mouth toward the stars and started to laugh, a jittery explosion of a sound. The pigeon didn't move though, just fluttered there watching.

AVA

2017

After a few days in the hospital, my mother is much improved, sitting up and eating; she's no longer a fall risk and she's been back and forth to the bathroom on her own.

She doesn't mention the house or Grandma and I'm relieved.

By lunchtime she says she feels cooped up, so I order a wheelchair and steer her around the pavilion downstairs. We pass the Peet's, the gift shop, the Get Well balloons and the inspirational paperbacks in the windows. I'd draped her in a backward gown to cover her ass and she hasn't washed her face or brushed her teeth in days. Still she looks like my mama, skin glowing, eyes bright. I'd brought a scarf from home to wrap her dredlocks away from her face. As I roll her outside, she drags her fingertips through every flowerbed and blade of grass, and it's like having a baby: in her presence,

211

I see the world with new eyes too.

After a while we just sit. I fill her in on the meeting with the girls yesterday and she nods and smiles.

"That Hazel," she says. "I worry about her. Trinity is fine, she has her family; her mother had thirteen brothers and sisters, and they already have a schedule set up: one of them will be in the house every day. But Hazel, she has so much riding on that man, and I can already tell he's not going to come through." She pauses. "If I tell you something, will you believe me?" she asks.

"Sure, Mama," I say.

She shakes her head. "Never mind," she says.

I talk some more about the girls, that Brittany seems like she'll deliver first but that Thandie was more impatient for it.

"My grandmother's grandmother talks to me in here," she cuts in finally. "Josephine. She still looks just like that picture I gave you."

"Oh?" I turn to her but I am not surprised. She talks like this from time to time.

She nods. "So clear it's like she's really there. She's telling me things too. Stories she never told my grandmother when she was alive. My grandmother would beg her, but she wouldn't say a word." She pauses

212

again. "People are so afraid of hauntings but I pray for them. Lord, clear me out so I can be one with all that have lived through me. There are the sweet hauntings, the tender ones you yearn for. Just one minute with the great beyond, I beg of him, and now he's starting to respond." She looks older as she's saying this, more unhinged than inspired, and I find myself leaning back, away from her.

"You feeling okay, Mama? You seem tired." I stand to wheel her back to her room, but she shushes me.

"She made her own jam," she says. "People would come to her from miles around to sample it. They'd spread it on biscuits but they'd spread it on rice and gravy too, it was that good. Any base would do as long as it would allow the taste of the juice, but it wasn't runny either, more like a pudding than anything, the fruit clumped in perfect little knots. She ran her own farm, even after her husband died. She had people to work for her, but up until she was too old to do it, she would be the one to milk the cows first thing in the morning; she let the renters draw on her butter. She never forgot how to do that work, she never forgot who she was doing it for, even though it was her farm, even though she could read and write." My mother whispers the next part: "She talked to spirits, you know. She was a woman who could fix things. She —"

"But it's over," I add. My mother has always seen through the veil between worlds, always revealed her view, but I'm uncomfortable now. I can't put my finger on why.

She quiets, looks up at me like she's realizing something.

"It's over now," I repeat.

"Maybe," she says. "Maybe."

That night, my mother's hemoglobin levels go up. The nurse calls me at 3 a.m. because she's pointing at people in her room who aren't there, shouting at them to leave her be, but the doctor chalks it up to too much ammonia in her blood, gives her a laxative, and all is well.

Grandma Martha is still on a high from my mother's visit and she's managed to organize a meeting with her book group. This month's choice is a fictionalized account of the first black girls' experiences integrating New Orleans schools. I've never read it myself, but saw from the jacket that it's written by a white woman. Grandma Martha had me suggest a casual meal to Binh to guide the conversation. He's chosen chili and cornbread, and I can smell the green peppers and onions, the tomato gravy and the beef.

"You ready for this?" I ask Grandma, as I

help her pick out a simple button-down and pants. She's been doing well. Most likely she'd be able to select something reasonable herself, but you never know. "It's a long two hours, and you know how some of those women can talk," I add.

She laughs at that. "Especially Marilynn," she says. "She never says anything important, just drones on and on. Doesn't she think other people might have an opinion? She doesn't care. And then Rose won't even have read the book," she goes on. "I swear she's just here for the crudités."

"I'd be too, I don't blame her, that and the pigs in a blanket."

The women gather slowly over the hour and mingle in the parlor until everyone has arrived. Marilynn and Rose, who have drivers; Anne, who has worked at an antique shop since her husband died in debt; and Patsy, who sells jewelry for fun, fake diamonds and gold that she would never wear but she's so successful at it she's started to earn more than her husband. They're dressed just like Grandma used to, in gingham shirts and ankle-length pants and fresh pedicures peeking out of their braided slides. They wear fleur-de-lis necklaces, carry monogrammed purses, push their designer glasses up on their noses, and they drink more Chardonnay than they eat. More than anything, they are all so happy to see me. It seems to elevate them as much as the alcohol does that I'm there.

Patsy says, "You're a good girl, taking care of your grandmother when she needs you."

And Anne says, "That's right. Blood is thicker than water."

When it's time to move I help Grandma to her seat. I take her hand and can feel it shaking.

"It's okay," I tell her so no one can hear, and she squeezes it back.

She sits and flips through the pages of the hardcover. As the host, she's supposed to speak first, and I don't know how much her friends know about her decline, or if her decline will even be relevant today. She doesn't speak for a while, just flipping the pages. I am sitting on the sofa scrolling Facebook, mostly peering out over the phone to see if I am needed. I start to stand just as Patsy exclaims that the part she loved most was the scene where the white teacher punishes the kids in the class who have pushed the little black girl into the mud.

"The way she held that child after," she says. "The way she continued to teach her alone. That's what we need. That's what we're missing."

Another lady agrees, but she wonders where the other supporters were. She saw the angry women who stood in lines outside the school each morning, yelling and carrying on, and it made her sick, but where were the ladies who were on the right side of history? Surely they were there, just like they're here now. The author should have paid more attention to that side.

Several times Grandma starts conversations that end up meandering. I notice her overuse of the phrase *in other words,* but she has trouble finding the other words even. Each time I see her struggle, I hurry over to her with some unnecessary errand to distract attention from her flailing. I replace her napkin or add more fruit to her side dish, switch out her silverware. When she starts talking about the Dufrene girls again, how coveted they were, and how precious, I head over with a pitcher of water. I start to fill her glass, and she moves it from my aim just as the water begins to flow.

"Goddamnit," she shouts as it hits her lap. "Can't you do anything right?"

She stands and more liquid spills to the hardwood.

"Calm down, Martha." Patsy reaches for napkins.

"She's supposed to be good help, but she's

causing more trouble than anything," Grandma goes on. I step back. Patsy pats Grandma's pants down. Anne stands up behind me and rubs my back, but I move away from her until I've separated from all of them and am on the bottom stair. I stand on it for a while clutching the railing, watching them fuss over Grandma. I have a tough feeling in my chest like meat stuck between my teeth and I'm waiting on one of them to say something that will retrieve it. But they don't and eventually I turn and walk away.

Upstairs, I sit on the edge of my bed and listen to the rest of the meeting. Grandma has gotten her steam back now. She's talking about how well the girls who integrated ended up doing: "Their success has to count for something." She's pointing out how much has changed. "Look at King," I hear her say, "nobody gives him any trouble." I think about what my mama has said, that there are versions of ourselves, there are versions of ourselves even within ourselves. In another house, in another moment, I might go down there and spout off what I learned in an African American studies class at Xavier my fifth year. I might whisper to them that I have a suspicion some of them would be on the sidelines barking at those little girls on their way to school. I might put Grandma to shame, but as it is, I stay where I'm seated. I take out my phone to call my mother, I even dial the digits, but I don't want to burden her. I don't want to hear *I told you so.*

My mother's sisters and I decide to throw a welcome-home party for my mother, and I am glad to get the break from Martha. It has been a few days since her outburst, and though she apologized, it still weighs on me. I counted the money last night, and I am only $7,000 short of my goal. Two months will fly by, I tell myself. I even go online today to look at townhomes.

About fifty people cram in my mother's house, some hanging over the kitchen counter scooping dip onto lime Tostitos, some sipping white wine on lounge chairs outside. I busy myself with the food: I miss cooking, stewing pork in a Crock-Pot, sprinkling garlic and slathering honey on a whole red fish, patting butter inside flour pockets for homemade biscuits, and everybody knows it doesn't make sense to cook jambalaya from scratch when Zatarain's hits for $1.59 a box. My mother washes tomatoes and cucumbers from her garden for a salad. We line the serving dishes out on her counter, and when it's time to eat, the room goes silent, except for the occasional grunt, like an extension of the grace my mother said before the meal. Everybody, I mean every single one of my relatives, gets up for a second serving.

I sit between my mother's sisters, and they tell me how proud they are of me, that they've heard King is in a better school, that we're looking at houses. It doesn't all feel true but I soak in the praise anyway.

Once we've eaten, we clear the tables and chairs from the center of the living room and turn on the music. Somebody suggests a dance competition, and mostly my cousins are doing the Beanie Weanie and the Jubilee, but some of their kids cut in with the Nae Nae and the Wobble.

I hear cheering break through every now and then and calls for my drunk Aunt Betty to sit down.

There is watermelon punch some of the uncles have snuck brown liquor into and babies are running from arm to arm. At some point in the night, my aunt slides a chocolate Bundt cake out of the oven, and we sing Stevie Wonder's version of "Happy Birthday" to my cousin who turned twenty-five two weeks earlier. There's only one candle in the cake, and we can't even find a lighter until my uncle who always smells like trees whips a BIC out of his pocket.

As we're slicing the cake, I notice King isn't there. I walk through the house, then outside the screen door, and see him sitting on the swing on the patio. It's been dark but my mother has old-school lanterns set up along the carport and they light up his face enough for me to see he's disappointed I've interrupted his flow. He has that phone out and he's FaceTiming with Harper again. Snippets of their conversation pop through, the parts I can understand:

"You don't know Eric? I have to introduce you. He's sooo cool." This from the girl.

"Nah, I don't know Eric. Does he know me?" This from my son.

I shake my head and sit next to him, half my face in the screen, all awkward, until he tells her he has to go.

Once he's hung up, I play-slap him.

"Boy, we're at a party. You just saw that girl. She can wait."

"I know, Mama."

"You know, huh?"

He's cheesing. It worries me, this relationship, but I've had a few drinks, and he seems so happy. I sigh. "You like her, huh?" I ask.

He nods. "She all right."

"All right? You can't even hang with your family? How often do you see Chase and Leah? They in there asking about you, and you out here on the phone with her."

"She's nice, Mama," he says.

"She must be real nice."

"I didn't want to move, you know," he cuts me off with a burst of energy that was not of the original conversation.

"I know," I say, and I feel my guilt rising because we're going to have to start all over again soon.

"Nah, it's cool. I don't mean it like that," he seems to sense my sadness. "I'm just saying she made it easy on me. She introduced me to everybody. She thinks I'm the funniest kid she ever met, she tells me that." He pauses. "I told her about Daddy, and she said it was his loss, not coming around."

"I told you that too," I say.

"Yeah, but I believe it when she says it," he says. "Now I'm glad we're here." He pauses. "If we hadn't come, I never would have met her."

We stay out there on the swing for some time. Christmas is around the corner, light jacket weather, but I left mine inside. Still, I have my hand on his thigh and I don't say a word.

After a while, we go back in and finish cleaning up. My mother's sisters are in the kitchen drying dishes. The rest of the family is crowded in the living room, the older relatives on the sofas, the younger ones at their feet. My mother sits on an armchair in the corner of the room; she's speaking quietly; I don't hear everything she's saying at first, but I can glean from the fragments that she's talking about Josephine.

"I've been seeing her, you know," she says. "Since I got out of the hospital."

The room quiets. Here we go again.

"Most of the time she's sitting at a round kitchen table," she goes on. "Laughing, smiling. Other times, she's younger, and she's being chased. I believe she's trying to tell me something."

My mother looks over at me. I was just about to wipe down the counters, but I stop, the dishrag limp in my hand.

"To warn me about something," my mother goes on. "About someone."

Her eyes are locked with mine. I look away.

"It's such a clear image," she goes on, "visions you wouldn't believe if I told you. A wide swamp, and deep inside it, patches of dry land. And then it's like she's on a levee, with men behind her. Two men riding two horses the same shade of brown."

I tense up even more, hearing her stir up the dreams I've had, so much so some details come back to me that I hadn't remembered seeing myself.

"The swamps, the men, the horses, the screams, the chase," she repeats. "I never thought about how they made it out. You know, slavery. I never thought about how exactly they freed themselves. I guess I assumed they lived past its ending, and they were free that way, but now, well, now I don't know what to think. The pictures, they're so vivid, I can smell the dirty water, I can taste the rodents they fried, I can hear the horses at their feet. And well, now, now I'm starting to think she escaped."

"That sounds like a movie," one of my mother's sisters cuts in from the kitchen.

I notice some of my cousins smirking. Some people think my mother is crazy when she talks like this, but I'm not one of them. I remember that drawer she kept with all of her clients' wishes, with all of her own, and every single thing she'd written down had come to pass. For that reason, I tell King to put on his shoes. In true black party fashion, it takes forty minutes to kiss everybody and pack up plates. My mother asks several times why we don't just spend the night, but I tell her I'm tired. Of course it's not that. It's one thing if she's envisioning a house for King, a new car for me; we could use all that, but the warnings — well, shit, I have enough on my plate.

JOSEPHINE

1924

I wait for Charlotte the next day. The day after that and the day after that too, but she doesn't come. It's been a week since my fallout with Major and Eliza, and I have stopped expecting them. I go days without seeing another face, and as much as I had feared loneliness, I find when it comes to pass, I have enough memories stored up on the inside to more than meet it. I fill my day. I spend more time with the Word. My favorite: *Thus saith the Lord; Cursed be the man that trusteth in man, and maketh flesh his arm, and whose heart departeth from the Lord. For he shall be like the heath in the desert, and shall not see when good cometh; but shall inhabit the parched places in the wilderness, in a salt land and not inhabited. Blessed is the man that trusteth in the Lord, and whose hope the Lord is. For he shall be as a tree planted by the waters, and that spreadeth out her roots by the river, and shall not see when heat cometh, but her leaf shall be green; and shall not be careful in the year of drought, neither shall cease from yielding fruit.*

I sit, travel into myself. There is that woman I always see. I try to avoid her, but as my eyes close, she is back more and more. She doesn't look like me, her skin is firmer and her hair is longer, but when I think, it comes out in her mind, and when I am soothed, she is the one to smile.

I knit. I take my meals, then have a walk around the property. Isaiah would be so proud of all that had come from those first two acres. Much of it he had seen before he left us, but some of it he hadn't. Sometimes I think I can sense him in the fields, stretching the tassels or carrying the pollen to the silks.

When I get back inside, it is time to start dinner, and it is lonely at first chopping seasoning for food no one else will taste, but I get used to that too, and I make a point of setting up the plate just so, the way I'd imagine Eliza doing it, even if it is for my eyes only.

When Jericho walks in, I feel like I am being jolted back into the living world.

"You scared me, stranger," I say. "What

happened? I get into it with Eliza, I get into it with all of y'all, huh?"

He doesn't say anything, and I look up and see he has been crying.

"What is it?" I stand up as fast as my old bones allow.

"I told you it was going to happen." He slumps into a chair across from me.

"You told me what, Jericho?" I am standing over him, my voice rising. "You told me what?" I repeat when he still doesn't respond.

"She's pregnant," he says. "Eliza is pregnant. They're going to have their own baby now and everybody's going to forget about me."

I try to control my own joy while I calm him. I would have thought I'd be reacting the same as he is, but I hadn't known how hungry I was for another member of my bloodline to come through. I will never get my mama back, not on this earth, probably my daughters neither, and it is not like the new life fills the holes they left, but it moves my gaze so I focus on the high times, when Mama carried me in from the rain and my head rested on her shoulder. Or one night, when grace stopped me in my tracks, my daughter moved a stone from one hand to the other and demanded for hours that I guess which fist it was in.

"It's going to be all right," I say.

"No, it's not. No, it's not," he repeats. "That's why I haven't come by. I didn't want to talk to anybody, not even you."

"It's going to be all right, baby. You're going to find it's going to be different, and you'll do well to not compare it to the past, but the thing is you'll find it's better too, better in ways you never would have expected," and he nods but he is still crying, his head down on his forearm.

"As much as it's theirs, it's going to be yours too," I say.

His eyes seem to light up at that. He is hearing me, at least some.

"You ever think about it that way?" I go on.

He shakes his head.

"As much as it's their baby, it's going to be yours too."

After I calm Jericho, I set to knitting: booties and bonnets, blankets and hats. My spirit tells me it is a girl and she'll be born in winter; she'll need wool sweaters, and why not stitch roses onto their pockets?

I tell everybody I see. When I take my walks, I pass out frozen cups for the workers, sit with Theron while he slurps the

231

sugar and explain to him that Isaiah told me it was a girl, that there was a curly head of hair he pointed to in a dream, and I couldn't see the face but he'd said, *Just look at her.* I don't tell him the girl would make up for the daughters who have left me. I don't feel the need to mention that part.

Whatever issue I take with Eliza flits off after that. I sit with her every day. Her own mother works, and she isn't much of a caretaker, but Eliza has terrible nausea in the first months and can barely get out of bed. Corn patties settle her stomach best, and I stand over the stove frying batch after batch. At first we don't say much to each other. I read my favorite pieces of the Bible, and she doesn't object, but she doesn't tell me to go on either. One day, out of frustration, I lay the book down.

"You're going to have to talk to me," I say. "If I'm going to be sitting here, you're going to have to at least tell me a kind word. I know you're mad about Major, about me giving Aristide's son that job, but if you only knew what it was like for me and my husband, for Aristide, and I couldn't look at myself in the mirror if I didn't take care of his child. I couldn't."

She nods. Her head is shifted to the left and I see a tear drop down the side of her

232

face. "It's not that," she says. "I know why you gave him that job."

I hesitate. "So you've come around then?" I ask.

She shakes her head. "I always knew why. But I'm a wife now, and my mother says I have to stand by Major. Problem is he's taken to heeding my brother's advice. And my brother's heard himself called fool so much, he responds to the word on the street."

I laugh. "Then why you being like this?" I ask.

She shakes her head, looks away. "I hate the way I am now," she says. "Dependent. If I need to piss, you gotta know about it." She throws her hands up. "It's just not what I'm used to, and I don't know if I'm going to be able to abide it."

"Well, you know you're going to abide it," I say. "That's the only thing you do know."

She doesn't answer, just keeps talking, looking away. "My grandmother took a year to die. Every morning we got up, the preacher said it would be the last day, but it went on like that for a full year. Got so bad, the day she actually did pass, nobody believed it. We hired our neighbor to sit with her so we could go to a sorority dinner, and we got back and the breath had left her body. My neighbor met us at the door, took one look at us, said without any pity, "She's gone." She blamed us, see, for leaving somebody so sick and shut-in, but we didn't know. We didn't know. She had hung in for so long, and for that reason, we didn't think another night would cost a thing."

"Sometimes it be's like that," I say. "That lady shouldn't have blamed you. Not something in our power to know. Everything is in his plan," I say. "Everything is in his plan," I repeat.

She nods. "I only say all that to say that I was the one to sit with her. I hadn't started teaching yet, and I was the only one home. More days than not, she had waste leaving her body from both ends, and I was the one to clean her up. I'd sit there and wish every minute of the day that the Lord would go on and take her. I never told anybody that. I cried like a baby when it happened, but sometimes I wonder if I wasn't the reason it did."

I pick up her hand on instinct, squeeze it. "I just told you you ain't got that power," I say. "Now, I just told you that."

She shakes her head. "Sitting here now just reminds me of it is all. Those days I wanted to rush past. I'm happy about this baby but I wonder if I deserve it, after what I did."

I keep quiet for a while. Most of the time, the most powerful part is bearing witness.

Then, "Nobody can watch someone else suffer, not someone you love. You wishing her gone, it was the right thing to do," I say.

She doesn't respond, just looks away, then she looks back, and what she says surprises me in a way I'm rarely surprised these days.

"I was wondering if you would deliver this baby, if you're able," she says. "I was going to get a doctor but I trust you more than anyone, and I thought it might be more special this way. I know you don't do it anymore, regular, at least."

I pause before I respond, though there's no way I'll say anything but yes.

"It's like falling asleep," I say. "Any way you could forget how?"

She shakes her head.

"That's how it is with me and babies."

After that, she asks me to tell her stories about Major. And I reach back in my mind's eye for as many visions as I can hold: he'd smear his face black with berries, crates of them; he loved to tell me about his dreams in the morning — always some monster was trying to attack him, but a streak of luck would save him, whales with no teeth or lions with no heart. I massage her feet until I see her eyes drift back, and I don't let her stand to put the dishes in the sink or to wash, and I say a prayer over her every day before I leave because it is what I wished someone had done for me. My only daughters are miles away, and I'd never stand at the bottom of their bed and watch them give over to the force of life. Not ever, but I could do it now, and it wasn't so much that I was pretending she was one of them, it wouldn't have been possible. My own children were a sturdy brown, as wide-hipped and broad-shouldered as I am, but it was that I brought her into the fold of my heart reserved for only them, and when I look at her now, I see one of my own all of a sudden, and my life blends into hers. It has become my responsibility to see her through.

Jericho is coming around. I dull my excitement when I am with him. I dwell on the parts of my old stories that light him up, I make his favorite foods: long spaghetti noodles with cheese, turkey necks with rice and gravy. It will be a sister, I tell him, and you'll have to protect her. When Eliza sees how much you love her, she'll love you all the more; you'll smell like rose water to her.

And Major — each time I look at him, all

his incarnations spring up at me at once. I see him spitting up on me at church in his white Easter outfit, choking on a fish bone, and I thought I'd lost him. Or when he handed me the baby from his first wife, looking so much like his daddy when I gave Isaiah my own children, and all of those images skip over each other and meld together into this one moment, and it is too much, I tell you it is too much.

Crying wasn't something I brought into this free world. When I stepped foot off that plantation, I said that it wouldn't follow me. It was one way to divide the past from the present, but if I hadn't drawn that line for myself, I'd have let loose now not only for joy but for the fullness of life, the breadth of it, the uncanny way it has of bringing everything back around, all the heartache you experienced served to you as something unrecognizable.

My spirit is so full that when the white woman comes back, I don't catch myself, I don't take a moment to just listen.

She is hesitant as ever at first. The mark around her eye has healed, but it is so fresh in my memory I still see it there as she lingers by the door.

"You know by now you ought to just come in," I say.

She is still standing by the door.

"You gotta know by now to just walk in," I repeat, and she moves, slowly, but she moves.

"How have you been, stranger?" I ask once she is seated. "Keeping yourself busy, huh?"

She nods. "I joined a new group," she says. "A women's organization. You'd be proud of me. I had to force myself to speak up so they'd hear my name during introductions, but before the meeting was out, I'd signed up to be treasurer."

Oh, well, look at God.

"That's great, sweetie," I say.

"Yes, I thought about you. I thought, *What would Josephine do?* Then I thought, *Josephine sure would be proud of me.* It's not a hard position; somebody's child could probably do it, but the lady before me got pregnant and has three little ones already, and she needed a break. Can you imagine? Four little children?" She is quiet again. "Anyway, I went to school until the eighth grade, and I followed the old lady's system pretty well. I think they'll be pleased with my work, hope they'll be."

"I'm sure they'll be rightly pleased, Charlotte," I say. "I'm so proud of you," I say again.

I almost don't say the next thing, I know better than anyone not to, but I am concerned. "And Vern?" I ask. "Things going better with him?"

"It's good to stay busy," she says, not answering the question but answering it too. "He's trying. I brought him in the group too, the same one I'm in, but the men's branch, of course, and it helps his mood to be social. He has people to talk to, ways of reordering himself. He's not as angry when he gets home, you know? Yes, I suppose things are better."

That's when I say in the same lilt I'd shared it with the others that my daughter-in-law is with child, and I can't contain myself I am so fit to burst.

I still don't catch myself until the silence. I look over at her. Everyone else had hit me with sound immediately; I hadn't had a moment in between my joy and their own, but here it stalls.

"Oh," she says. And she grabs her own stomach, looking like she is taking sick.

She doesn't say anything for a while, just runs her dirty-nailed fingers across my table cloth back and forth and back and forth.

"Did you have to help her?" she asks finally.

I shake my head. "She's young, healthy.

They only been married a few months. I'm sorry," I say finally, "not for my blessing, God gave that to me, and I receive it, but I'm sorry for your pain, I am. You're in an unfortunate position, and I'm sorry for you."

She mutters something.

"What's that?" I can't hear it, and the high part of my mind tells me to let it pass, it wasn't for me, but the other part rules me sometimes. "Say that again," I say.

"I said, 'not sorry enough to help it.' " She is louder this time. She has grown bolder in the last few weeks, and I remember her women's group, that she had said she was treasurer. Some people can't handle power; if it is placed over a bruised spirit, it corrodes it; when the landing is soft and whole, it is like plopping seeds in dirt. "I almost forgot. We have a meeting at two." She looks down, then up again. "I just wanted to stop by and let you know about me."

"Well, I'm glad you did, Charlotte. Don't be a stranger now," I say, and she gives me a hug before I can object, a quick tap more than anything, and then she gets up and walks off without saying a word. Her head is up, I notice. In all the time I've known her, she walked with her eyes on her shoes, but this time her head is up, and I can feel her skin, the sticky heat, against me long after she is gone.

And with the feel of the skin comes the rest of it.

JOSEPHINE

1855

I hadn't seen Miss Sally much since we stopped the bleeding. Every time I'd have a free minute away from folding the linens or minding the younger children, Missus would add a cover sheet to my pile or point at the dust on her bureau. She was getting bigger and she either needed to be repositioned or to have her feet lifted on the hour. The whole while I waited on her she'd complain, first about the heat, then when she'd get bored of that, she'd drift over to her mother, but all of that was just a circling over a known target and that target was Tom.

"Normally I can't keep him off me," she said that day. "But now, since I'm carrying, he hasn't laid a finger on me. Some men can go without. My mama taught me that, some men can, but Tom's not one of them, he just isn't."

I was filling a basin with heated water, waiting on it to cool.

"Your mother, what was she up to last night?" she added. My finger was an inch into the water. It wasn't too hot, but I knew Missus. She liked it almost cold. Sometimes I thought we wasted our time boiling it.

"My mother?" I asked. I tried not to show my nervousness. The draw was just days away and the last thing we needed was more eyes on Mama.

"She cooked me my supper, sat with me while I ate it. Then we went to sleep," I said.

"You sure about that, girl?" she asked.

"Yes, ma'am," I said.

Then I helped her out of her petticoat and into the water.

I took Mama aside as soon as I could to warn her, but she brushed it off.

"She's a weak woman," she said, "reaching for a hold on something so she won't fall down."

I brought it up again the night of the drawing, but Mama said, "I don't want to hear nothing about no Missus tonight," as we walked the three hundred yards to the swamp. Tom had company and Mama had to wait longer to clear their plates, so we were the last to arrive at the crossroads.

The others shuffled their feet in a circle around the altar, patting their thighs, rolling their necks, jerking their shoulders, and swinging their hips. They were singing too, and when they saw us, they shouted louder, their mouths agape:

Oh brothers will you meet me,
Oh brothers will you meet me,
Oh brothers will you meet me,
On Canaan's happy shore?

Daddy stood, burst into the middle of the circle, hopping around on one foot, then the other. With his hands behind his back, he jerked his upper body back and forth, breathing out on the upswing, then in, until I thought he might fall out.

By the grace of God I'll meet you,
By the grace of God I'll meet you,
By the grace of God I'll meet you,
On Canaan's happy shore.

He turned toward the altar, then floated more than walked over, and when he reached it, he bowed. The song softened. The dance slowed. Mama turned to face us.

"Call those things which be not as though they were."

"Call those things which be not as though they were," we repeated, our palms up.

"Call those things which be not as though they were," Mama said again.

And we shouted it out after her.

"Now take a deep breath, in and out. In and out. Close your eyes. Turn your vision inside out. Drift into a softer part of your mind, the part you don't show nobody, I mean nobody, the part that remembers coming into this world, that knows the exact minute you're going out. That's the part I want you to unlock, that's the part I want you to use, to consider your mamas, to set your mind on her face. Was it wrinkled? Black? How many teeth did she have when she smiled? Or remember your lady, your man, your child. You ain't got none of those? That's all right. If you don't have none of those, think about your breath. You didn't tell your heart to pump, did you? Your lungs to fold in and out? Something inside you just knew. Who was it? Who was it? You know who it was. It was the part of you that's going to linger when we're all dead and gone. It's the part of you that remembers walking free, breathing free air, bearing free children. It's the spirit of God that lives inside you. It's the spirit of your ancestors guiding and protecting you. Give thanks to it. Tell it hello. See if you can give yourself over to it, see if it will order your mind, take charge of your body, see if you can tell it to help you fly on out of here."

As she spoke, the singing started up again, low at first.

Oh brothers will you meet me,
Oh brothers will you meet me,
Oh brothers will you meet me,
On Canaan's happy shore?

Then it rose higher still.

By the grace of God I'll meet you,
By the grace of God I'll meet you,
By the grace of God I'll meet you,
On Canaan's happy shore.

Oh brothers will you meet me,
Oh brothers will you meet me,
Oh brothers will you meet me,
On Canaan's happy shore?

By the grace of God I'll meet you,
By the grace of God I'll meet you,
By the grace of God I'll meet you,
On Canaan's happy shore.

Mama rang the bell, and we opened our eyes. She had placed a basket on the altar too, and she held it up, jingled it. Then she reached in and pulled out a rock so small I could barely see it before she lifted it to her eye. Without even twisting her face, she turned it toward us, but I could read the answer in her still expression; she was staying.

No matter, she walked through the circle with the basket outstretched like all her hopes hadn't been aimed at this one night. The others reached in. Earl would stay, then Miss Bertha, Agatha, Elijah, Belle, and I started to wonder if it was a mistake, if the mark of the star hadn't been included. All the while we kept singing, our voices rising in a new, great rush.

By the grace of God I'll meet you,
On Canaan's happy shore.

There were only three people left. Lionel, then Seamus, then Daddy, and I wondered if it would be Lionel or Seamus. Lionel had a family in the field, and they could use the break more than Seamus, who was light as pancake batter.

There was a rustle in the grass just beyond us, and we knew to make the song rise higher because nothing scared white folks off like the Holy Spirit. Seamus was next to the altar and he swept its contents onto the ground. Mama slipped the remaining rocks in her skirt. She crept toward the sound. We kept singing, our eyes facing forward until I felt him. I turned. Jupiter. He wasn't supposed to be here. I looked to Daddy to object but he kept singing, bracing for his turn. Jupiter knelt beside me like it was where he sat each week, and he started telling me things without his mouth moving, that we were the chosen ones and we were free, we were born to be free and no one was going to take it from us any longer and we weren't just running through the tunnel, legs rolling, arms flapping, we had run, we had flown, and we were already looking back weeping because so much was lost, but it was over now and I could see it with him there; he cleared out a haze in front of our faces and if I squinted hard enough, I could see myself but it was not myself, it was a woman, that same pretty, pretty woman I always saw, and she was standing alone but her daughter was walking back toward her.

Seamus pulled, then Lionel, and it was neither.

It was Daddy's turn next.

Fred started shouting before Daddy even pulled. "You're fixing it for your man, for your family. Ain't nobody that lucky."

Jupiter looked over at him, and just like that Fred was quiet. Daddy pulled, and when Mama nodded, the whole group burst into a cheer. They raised Daddy up on their shoulders. I looked up at him, then back at Mama; she was happy, hesitant, but happy. Even Jupiter seemed like Daddy pulling was his path out. I looked back up at Daddy; he was mouthing a new song I'd never heard before:

And he'll open the door
Yes, he'll open that door
And it won't be long
No, it won't be long
Up beyond the velvet pass
below the reeds
and through the haunted grass
I'll press on to the largest star
that will lead me on

He was mouthing it, and he was fisting the air, but he wasn't smiling.

When we got back in the house after the draw, we could still hear the merriment in the quarters. Mama said that when you spent months imagining another person's freedom, homing in on it, desiring it with the beat of your heart, you forgot you were separate. The others were happy for Daddy, yes, but they had become Daddy too.

Mama and Daddy sat at the table. "They always said you were lucky, Domingo, but twice in a row." Mama shook her head, which was in his lap, and he twirled a strand of her hair from the middle of her scalp where it was coarsest. "Never would have imagined it," she went on. "When I didn't pull, I just knew we weren't going." She paused. "I was disappointed because I had seen it, you know, even felt the hem of my dress swirling around my ankles, felt Josephine's hand in mine. But more than disappointed, I was confused, like maybe all of this, the preparation, the prayer, the belief, the visioning was for nothing, like maybe I was making it all up. You ever feel that way? You ever wonder that?"

Daddy paused, then he moved his hands out of her hair. "You saw me running beside you?" he asked.

"Of course I saw you running," she said.

He paused. "You sure it was me? Or was it Jupiter? I know he got it in his head to run too." He jumped up and Mama's head fell on the chair where he'd sat.

"Well, he can't run," she said, sitting up too. "He didn't draw the stone. He not as lucky as you are," but she said it like in a way she wished things were different.

Daddy was up in her face now. "You wanted it to be him, didn't you? Admit it." He was not hitting her — he never would — but it felt like he was, and I put my hands over my ears and I closed my eyes. I imagined myself as the woman I'd just seen. She had family, she wasn't with her family, the way I was with mine, but she had somebody, peering over her shoulder, tapping on a window, only the woman didn't know to let her in.

"I hardly know that man, you know that," Mama went on. "Get offa me with all that."

"Say it then, you're happy that I'm going with you. Just say it." But he wasn't threatening her as much as he was begging.

"Fine. I'm happy you're going with me. There." And she was crying now.

And Daddy wasn't crying, but he should have been, I could see a little boy inside his body weeping.

"Just quit it," I screamed. "Just quit it."

They ran over to me. They were extra sorry now. They rubbed my head and pressed it into their stomachs. They held each other's hands.

"We're going to all be together soon," Daddy said to me. "It's all going to be okay."

"We're together now, Daddy," I said, but

Mama and Daddy just looked at each other.

AVA

2017

A few days after my mother's welcome-home party, I am driving King home from Harper's when the phone rings. I look down and see it's not the first time. I've somehow missed five other calls from the same unknown number.

I answer. It's Juanita. Grandma Martha has been missing for hours. They've looked all over the house and are afraid she's snuck outside. They are most concerned about the streetcar tracks and Binh has offered to ride up and down St. Charles to make sure she isn't walking in the wrong direction up one. I speed through yellow lights and park at the house. Juanita is standing outside holding a flashlight, calling out Martha's name. King and I join her then decide to knock on the neighbors' doors.

We walk past Grandma's house, the street car tracks to our left, her neighbors' gas lamps shining to our right. Oak trees line the sidewalk, and their roots lift the pavement and forge inclines and drop-offs between each square. Traffic is slow this time of evening, and when cars slow down beside us, their drivers turn and look us up and down.

We are almost at Jefferson Avenue when we hear a muffled voice call out, "Nine-one-one, what's your emergency?"

It's Grandma's medical alert. King runs toward the sound and Juanita and I follow him. The voice is coming from a double gallery house a couple of blocks from Grandma's. Approaching it, I see the back gate is ajar. I hear the voice again, "Nine-one-one, what's your emergency?" We look through the crack the open gate makes and see Grandma huddled up in an oversized jacket between two bushes.

King runs to her.

Juanita and I are right behind him.

"Grandma," I say, when we reach her. She blinks a few times. The back door of the house is windowpaned. I can look through it and see a living area not unlike Grandma's, and I want to get out before the owner sees us too.

"Grandma," I repeat. "What are you doing out here?" I am angry at her still — I haven't forgotten the incident with her book group — but I am relieved too, and I pull her toward me.

"I was looking for the cabins," she says, standing. Her knuckles are scraped and bloodied from the thorns. The owner of the house has come, and I try to wave at him, motion to somehow explain the situation, but I see him reach for his phone.

I tell King to grab her other side, and we hustle out to the sidewalk. The whole while, Grandma is talking nonsense.

"I saw the fields but I didn't see the cabins," she says. "I was looking to apologize to you again, for the other day, but I didn't see the cabins."

"Okay, Grandma," I say, "don't worry about it. It's okay."

It is a short walk to her house and I set her up at the dining room table with a cup of tea.

Juanita whispers to me, "She's getting worse, hallucinating now. I've seen it all before. It's normal," she says. "But she can't be alone anymore."

"Absolutely not," I say. I walk back up to Grandma and rub her shoulder. "We're so glad you're safe, Grandma."

"Oh yes, I only wonder, who was that handsome colored boy?"

When we get to the house, we practice breathing techniques and visualization exercises, help Hazel draft a birth plan.

She is in better spirits. She says she's starting to get excited without the dread. Her baby daddy is back in the picture. He was just getting nervous, that's all. It's a lot on him, and he retreats, but they talked about ways of coming together when they're stressed, and he's on board.

I don't need to look at my mother to know she's not impressed.

"Whether he's there or not, you can do this, Hazel," she says.

"I know, Miss Gladys, I'm just saying he's going to be there this time."

My mother looks at her hard until Hazel meets her eye. "Whether he's there or not, Hazel," she says again.

Hazel looks away, not unlike the way I would when I was a child and my mother would chastise me. It's quiet for a while, with Hazel looking down and my mother staring at her, until I stand.

"How are you feeling, Mama?" I ask, to change the subject. "You look good."

"Better than ever," she sings out. "I'm just glad I made it out of the hospital without catching pneumonia. In my condition, something like that could put me in the ground."

We talk about King and his lil' beige friend, as my mama calls her.

"Aww, poor baby," Hazel says. "I got some friends I could hook him up with. Some of them don't have kids yet."

"Girl, stop," I say, laughing, though I might consider it.

My mother asks about Grandma for the first time since she left the hospital, and I tell her I started looking at townhomes. I have a little while before I have enough for the down payment, but I'm getting there. It will fly by.

Several times I start to say more, about the previous night, how Grandma wandered off for the first time, how I'd had to increase Juanita's hours, but I'm embarrassed that I'm even in this situation in the first place, that I let it go so far; it has felt so good to be needed by Hazel, and I don't want her looking down at me.

My mother doesn't need to hear me say it. "Come home," she says.

"Ma, I keep telling you —" I start.

"I had another vision last night."

"Yes, I know, the swamps," I say.

She shakes her head. "It was different this time," she says. "I'm telling you, I saw a house, and it was just like the house you're

259

in. The oaks leaning over it, the shutters, the walkway leading up."

"Mama." The word comes out sharper than I intend. "I got this," I say again, softer this time.

It's quiet for a while, even more awkward than when Hazel and my mother were getting into it. I can see Hazel pull out her phone. She's probably not even doing anything on it, just biding the time before we get up out of there.

My mother comes in again to break the silence, like the conversation had never lapsed. "I hear you," she says. "But just know you don't need to prove anything. Come home, and look from home. I don't want to bind you there, I know you have your own life. But you'll feel better, Ava, if you're looking from a place of power."

The rest of the week moves slowly. King is still mad at me for mentioning moving, but there's an end-of-semester ceremony at his school, and he takes home the Model of Excellence award for achievement. After the program, I rush to the back to meet him. I notice that Harper is standing with another boy, a white boy with blond hair and braces, taking photos. The two use their bodies like dividers, and King and Claire skirt the edge of the group. When the photo is done, Harper asks King if he wants to go to Reginelli's with them, and he says no, he's tired.

We walk to our car and head home. Several times at red lights, I look back at him.

"I couldn't be prouder of you," I say more than once.

"I know," he says.

"No, really, it's a new school, a more rigorous one at that, but you didn't let it faze you. You went in and you shined, in every way," I add, but he still faces the window.

I start to ask him if something's wrong, if it's the move or something else, but I can tell he's not in the mood. When we get to the house, I expect him to go straight upstairs, but he doesn't. He and I sit in the living room for a while. Finally he turns to me.

"I was thinking maybe I could go to the skating rink, with Harper, just me and her, and you could drive us?" he asks.

I want him to feel better, and I know more change is waiting in this corner of his life, so I nod.

"This weekend?" he asks again.

"Okay," I say, and he kisses me on the cheek and runs upstairs.

■ ■ ■ ■

As the week plods on, my mother improves and even drives herself to the East to visit Hazel on her own. Grandma Martha has been in fine spirits, reading during the day, dressing the way she did, and combing her hair back and snapping barrettes into it. It's not that I forget what has been, but her condition, my proximity to it, seems less pressing, and I wonder if I can't wait a little while longer. It would improve my prospects.

King and Harper firm their little plans. I half hoped a conflict would turn up. Taking my son on a date, sitting beside the girl's mama, making conversation, well, it's not the way I would want to spend my Saturday. Still, the morning of, he's as excited as I've ever seen him.

He walks downstairs in a Nike track suit I got him for Christmas and new True Flights that are still flashing white.

On the way to Metairie, he asks me to play his favorite songs: "Bad and Boujee," "That's What I Like," and I do, and we sing along the whole ride.

I'm talkin' trips to Puerto Rico

Say the word and we go
You can be my fleeka
Girl, I'll be a fleeko, mamacita
I will never make a promise that I can't
  keep

He's always been a talkative child but he's even more so today, rehashing the plot of *Baby Driver* and telling me about the bowl he carved for me in the woodshed at school, that it's still drying, but when I see it, I'm going to think a professional made it. He starts to whisper like somebody's listening: "I made something for Harper too, I have it with me." He roots through his pocket and pulls out a chain with a royal-blue glass pendant on the end of it.

"It's beautiful, baby," I say into the rearview.

He nods. "I'm going to give it to her today."

I pause. "You sure?" I ask. "It's so nice, you could keep it for —"

He stops me before I can finish. "I already decided, Mom," he says. "I'm going to give it to her today."

And when we pull into the parking lot, he runs in ahead of me, pointing to a white SUV Beamer behind him, shouting back, "That's them. That's her mom's car. She's

263

already there."

He's right. Harper's mother is inside helping Harper lace up her skates. After I pay for King, I sit with the mother at the refreshment stand. She talks more than I do. She's looking for private schools for Harper. The high schools in the area get questionable is the thing; she works hard, and Harper deserves the best. I watch the kids as she talks — King is a better skater, and he laps Harper, then when they're together again, he takes her hand and leads her. King dances while he glides, and Harper covers her mouth, pointing at him and giggling. I settle into the scene after a while. The mother wants to know what I do, and I tell her about Grandma, my old job with Mr. Jeff, that I've been trying out work as a doula.

"You're kidding," she says.

I shake my head.

"You're kidding," she repeats.

"No, why?" I say. "Are you one too or something?"

She shakes her head. "I wish," she says. "No, it's just that I had a doula with Harper. She lived with us for six weeks after too, took care of the baby. She was a saint. Her sister had committed suicide and she was a tough woman. She'd tell me what to do and I'd just respond, 'Yes, ma'am.' " She laughs. "I could see you being like that too," she says. "If you do become a doula, let me know. My younger sister is in a mom's group now. They're all looking for someone to night nurse."

I'm about to tell her that's not the kind of work I'm imagining when King walks back up, less animated than he was. He wants a soda so I hand him some change. He comes back, gulps it, then says he's ready to go.

"Where's Harper?" I ask, and he nods behind him. She's still on the rink. Some other little boy has rolled up. He looks familiar. I squint at him and realize it's that same kid from the program. I turn to Harper's mother for an explanation but she seems just as confused as I am. King is at the door before I can say goodbye and I hurry out to meet him in the parking lot. I know better than to ask questions this time.

I play his songs on the car ride home but he doesn't sing along. There's traffic, and the ride back to Grandma's is slow. We are about to turn onto St. Charles; I think he's gone to sleep when he speaks.

"How do you know if someone likes you as a friend or as more than that?" he asks. He's twisting his dredlocks like he does.

I was expecting something along those

lines but I still hadn't prepared for it.

"I don't know," I say. "It's a feeling you get I guess," I say after a while. "A special spark, a chemistry." I'm talking slowly. "A tender spot in your heart that's special for only that person," I go on.

"Well, then I guess I can't trust myself," he says. "Because I thought we had that." He whispers that part. "The whole time she had a crush on that kid, Eric; she told me just now. You were right about the necklace." He throws it down on the seat next to him. "About the whole thing I guess."

"I'm sorry, baby," I say. I pull up at Grandma's and hurry out of the car. I try to beat him to the house but he's ahead of me, bolting up the stairs.

I check on him twice, but he says he needs his space, and I pour myself a tall glass of wine to wait it out. Juanita is there tonight so I don't even look in on Grandma; though I feel guilty about that, I drown it out with Cabernet. A part of me wants to call Harper's mama and curse her out for letting her daughter lead my son on, and why wouldn't she want him? He is handsome, bright, hilarious. Everyone thinks so. It was probably his race, and a part of me is sad about that, but a bigger part is glad it's over. I had known that the situation wasn't headed anywhere safe, and maybe this is the best-case scenario, the least amount of hurt I could have expected.

It takes me a while to get upstairs, I feel so heavy and leaden, and when I do, I fall into a slumber so deep that when I wake up it feels like I've been out for many hours. It's still dark out though. I can see from the light filtering in from the hallway that Martha is in my doorway. I hear her shouting before I can make out what she says. And then it's clear.

"Thief," I hear her shouting. "Thief," she repeats. It takes a while for my eyes to adjust but soon I can see she's holding the necklace, the one she gave me when I first moved in.

"You gave that to me," I say, my voice groggy.

"I never thought it but there it is." She points at me. "The ladies were right to tell me to keep an eye on you."

She walks toward me and I cover my neck.

"Grandma, you gave that to me," I repeat. "Remember?"

"And to think I trusted you. To think I treated you like family and you betrayed me. You made me look like a fool."

"Grandma, get out," I yell.

"Not until you admit it," she says, and she

lunges over to me but she hits the bed and doubles over in the process. She goes limp on the comforter and begins to wail.

I get up, slide my robe on, and lift her hand to walk her back to her room.

"I'm so sorry," she whines as I hold her up. "I didn't mean it, don't leave me, don't leave me. Promise me you won't. Promise me you won't leave me by myself."

I tell her I won't just to move her. When I get her to her room, I help her into bed, then rummage through her medicine cabinet for a sedative.

I sit beside her until she settles down.

"We were the prettiest girls in the whole county," she says again.

"Um-hmm, Grandma," I say, but I am tired and I tune out the rest.

She passes out soon midsentence, and I leave, but I don't go back to my room. I stand outside King's instead; he has always been a deep sleeper. I go in farther and watch his chest rise and fall. I can't sleep, and as the sun's coming up, I peer through his window. I look for the pigeon but it's gone. There's something else though, some sort of mass hanging from the oak tree, the height of a person, the depth of one too. I open the window. I can make out where the head would be, bent sideways; down where the legs would fall, whatever's draped there seems to sway. I close the window back so fast I slam my finger, then scramble in the bed and pull King toward me. I lie like that until the sun is up. When King goes to pee and wash his face, I force myself back to the window for a peek. I pull the curtain, but it's nothing; of course it's nothing — thick clumps of dried Spanish moss dangling.

JOSEPHINE

1924

Everybody within a quarter mile hears the tree crack. I barely look up I am so engrossed in telling Theron about the dream I had the night before. "I saw her face," I say. "I saw her face." She's a yellow old thing, with coal-black ringlets, but she opened her lips to cry, and my mama's voice came out. I don't remember her words, and the more I concentrate on the memory, the further it recedes, but that is okay because I heard her voice. Theron may care, or he may just enjoy the slick red syrup melting off the ice I froze for him. I only know he is content, and because we are both in our own ways being soothed, we don't pay attention to the tree falling, not its fall nor our workers limbing from the branches' base.

That night at Major's, I am deep in the dressing and string beans I stewed, the chicken I baked in green onions, garlic, and orange juice when we hear the knock. Louis is there of course; he's gained ten pounds since Eliza's pregnancy. Not too much of my food he doesn't return for seconds on, sometimes thirds. He talks even more than he eats, starting off most sentences with *First of all* and *What you need to know is.* He doesn't do a whole lot else though. I've asked Eliza privately if he works, and I couldn't get a straight answer from her, just some rumbling about yes and no at the same time.

"It's Miss Link," Jericho says about the noise at the front door.

I shake my head. "Can't be Link, sounding like that." It is too heavy a sound for it to be her, too jolting and sharp.

Major walks to the door, eases it open.

My back is to him, but I can tell by Major's voice there's a white man on the other side of him. By the way he drops the bass, dulls the edges around his words, and of course he calls him *sir* the way I taught him.

The white man's words come out in sputters. "Uh, I hear tell, uh, one of your workers cut down my tree this morning."

That's when I stand up and turn around. It's Charlotte's husband.

"Is that right?" Major asks. It is like the

271

white man's nervousness steadies Major, and I want to tell him to slow down, there is strength in slowing down.

"Yeah, that's what the people are saying, that that tree fell on my line."

"I didn't hear nothing about a tree. Mama, you heard something about a tree?" He doesn't look backward when he asks me.

"Um-hmm, scraggly old thing. I didn't think to mention it." I walk to the door. "Only it's on our line. I got the deeds at my house," I say. "I usually carry them with me, sir, but I'm here taking care of my sick daughter-in-law, and I can get them as soon as I get home, carry them over to you."

When I mention the deeds, he gets red in the face like they do. I look down at his feet — the shoes Charlotte's mama said were so nice have seen better days.

"Oh, that won't be necessary. You say it was a small tree?"

"Scraggly old thing," I repeat.

"Well," he waves his hand at me. "I reckon there are plenty trees on that property. Maybe next time just check in with me. If something like that ever happens again."

"Yes, sir, we will." This from Major, and I am proud of him; there is that ever-present shame too that it has to go down this way, but it is slight. If I wasn't looking for it, I

272

wouldn't know it was there.

Eliza has already gone to bed. She only has two months left. She's not sick anymore, but she is accustomed to being a small woman, and now there are twenty pounds pulling her forward. It is the newness of the weight, the suddenness, that could trip her up; a fall this late could take the baby out, her too. A pregnant woman steps one foot into a graveyard.

The whole while Louis is just sitting there silent. It's unusual for him, but after a while of it, I assume for once he'll sit out. Then he clears his throat and reaches for his pipe like that's his mouthpiece. He lights it and takes a few puffs before he speaks.

"You let a man treat you like a dog too many times, you start to feel like one. Start barking. Scratching yourself, eating with your hands, roaming, growling. Might as well walk on four feet. Nah," he goes on, "can't nobody make you grovel. I don't like to see any man grovel," he repeats.

"Grovel?" I pause, searching for the right words. There are so many they want to rush out in misplaced order. "Grovel?" I repeat. "Lord, deliver me. Do you mean stay alive? You don't like to see a man protect himself and his family? You have any idea what would have happened if he hadn't done it

273

like I taught him?"

He shrugs. Jericho is watching us, trying to see which side he falls on, and I want to make it clear.

He is with me.

"All that might work in New Orleans, it may work if you so yellow you appear white like you, but this here is Resurrection, and I don't need to go to school to tell you with serious authority that you talk to a white man like you got some sense, and he'll blow your head open."

Jericho looks troubled, but he has to hear it that way. It's what it is.

I wait for Louis to say something more so I can repeat myself good enough for him to hear me, but he doesn't say a word, and after a while I get up and walk back to my own house. Charlotte is on her porch when I get there, looking straight ahead.

"I came by," she says. "But you weren't there. I figured I'd wait up, that you were with your people."

I nod.

"Vern told me about that tree. I hope he didn't scare y'all going all the way out there. Vern is a weak man." She is whispering now. "One of his friends got in his ear, told him he needed to stand up, but he's harmless."

I almost say *That mark on your eye don't*

274

prove he harmless, but I take the advice I just gave my son, and I nod.

"Thank you for saying so," I say.

"So I hope he didn't scare you."

"We'll be more careful next time," I say. It is the first time I have talked to her outside my kitchen, and something about it doesn't feel right. I am itching to get back inside.

"Maybe I can come by sometime. I been busy with my group, but maybe tomorrow."

"That'd be nice," I say, and I turn my back. I look out the window a half hour later, and she is still sitting on her porch, whistling.

The next morning, I am clearing my breakfast when Theron runs up.

"Somebody tore out the greens," he says. "There were two whole acres of 'em just sitting, ready to be plucked, and somebody ripped them out by the root, then shredded them apart."

"Or some *thing,*" I say. My eyes are still on my food. I hadn't gotten the plates cleared, but I was already thinking about lunch. Pulled pork with sweet tomato sauce, extra pickles, and I can taste the first bite.

"Can't be a thing. Can't be an animal tear 'em out that neat. Got to be a person."

That idea sends a chill through me, but I remain calm. It was Isaiah who taught me that people don't care what you do in a situation like this, only how.

"Go call Major," I say. "Let me get to my lunch." But when he is gone, and I am done stewing the meat and smashing the tomatoes, I have to set the sandwich aside. It's not the crops. They'll set us back to be sure, but it's the smell of the whole matter, not even cloaked, reeking and foretelling rot.

Major can smell it too. I can tell because he pretends it's not there.

"Nothing but a raccoon set through that trap," he says.

"You know well as I do wasn't no raccoon," I answer him.

We are standing side by side in the rows his daddy dug up when he was just a boy, and just as sure as I can see Major now, a man with swollen arms and a hard chest talking down to me, I can see him climbing on his daddy's back as Isaiah bent to sprinkle the seeds.

"Rows ain't as neat as Theron claimed is the thing. I could see how he thought that from the distance, but when you peer down at 'em real close you can see nothing but a raccoon scurried through there, maybe a rabbit. One or the other."

"And if it wasn't no rabbit. If it wasn't no raccoon, what would it be then? What would it mean for us?"

"Eliza ain't got but a few more weeks to be pregnant, Mama," he says then. He is tired of me, his voice says, and if I wasn't his mama, he'd be tired enough to throw me out.

"What that got to do with the cost of beans?"

"I don't have the energy to do it all," he says. "She a nervous wreck, this being her first time, and her mama ain't the nurturing type. I'm all she got. We all she got, and we got to stay calm through this, or it's going to take us out. We can't go borrowing trouble. You hear me?"

"I hear you, baby," I say.

"All right, Mama. I love you, you hear?" He takes my hand. It is not the way Jericho would do it. When he is a man he will still cradle my face and bury himself in me. You can know these things. But I'll take it from Major, I'll take it even though he doesn't stay for dinner that night, and when I ask him if I can come to help with Eliza, he says she's fine, that the two of them will manage just fine.

A week later the pig is dead. Not the other Hampshire but a good hog nonetheless, and they have taken all her good meat.

I walk right over to Major's.

"We need to apologize," I start before I even sit down.

"Apologize to who, Mama?"

"My neighbor. He the one killed that pig."

He nods. "And what you think we should say when we apologize? *We sho' is sorry fo' tryin' to be equal to youz, boss. We realizin' mo' and mo' every day that all we is is a bunch of rascally —.*"

"Hush up," I cut him off.

Louis is next to him snickering in his hands.

"Now, don't get smart with me, boy," I go on. "You not too old for me to backhand slap you. You know I'm not talking about doing all that," I go on. "I'm talking about going over there in a respectful manner. You can catch more flies with honey than vinegar, you know that. Maybe I'll address Charlotte first; I've spent some time with her. I might ask her what they want for that tree. Pay it and move on. No amount would be too much if we could move on."

He shakes his head. "I'm tired of being the bigger person with these people," he says. "I'm tired, Mama." I can see the weight of his exhaustion straining his spirit, and I feel guilty for bringing him in this world to bear it.

I put my hand on his back. "What was it your daddy used to say?" I ask. "You got to give respect to get it."

"They killed that good pig and you talking to me about respect."

Eliza walks up to comfort him, but he turns away from her, toward me.

"I'm sorry, Mama," he says. "I'm just tired. I'm just so, so tired. I'm tired of carrying it. I want somebody else to carry it for a minute. It never lets up. It's like somebody's fingers pinching me on the inside of my chest, and it won't ease up, it won't let me feel like a man. It won't never let me feel like a man. That's all I want is to go somewhere with my child, and feel whole, all the way, but it won't let me, but you got these white people out here not good enough to shine my shoes and they get to feel like there ain't no limit to what the world owes them." He pauses. "Jericho looks up to me, I can feel it. He always in my shadow and it should feel good but it wears on me 'cause I know one day he gon' look at me the way I looked at Daddy the first time I saw him for who he really was. And I can't bear it, Mama. I swear to God I can't bear it."

I nod. It is a feeling I've grown accustomed to. When I was a young girl I feared it, what it would do to me to grip his shoulder, to hold him back and let a white boy pass in front of him, to discipline him only for him to watch a white woman call me girl. The feeling has run its course now. It is what it has to be. There is no use pretending otherwise.

"What do you want me to do?" I ask.

He shrugs, his head in his hands. "I don't know, Mama," he says, "but I won't go to 'em, like we the ones did something wrong. I can't handle the thought of you doing that either. Maybe one of 'em will be man enough to come to me."

Eliza is holding his hand and nodding so strong up and down that I say okay. Her brother is right beside him and he doesn't say anything, but he doesn't have to. His words are streaming out of Major's mouth on their own accord.

I fix their dinner. Afterward I get up to present my banana pudding, sponge cake stacked throughout. I spoon it, and Louis only has four bowls before he leaves for his own house. It is so late I decide to just sleep on Jericho's bed, with him on the floor beside me. Tomorrow, I have to go see about a girl midway through her pregnancy, and Link had asked me to bake her an egg custard pie. I can taste the sweet filling, firm though, the butter in the crust as I drift off. When the smoke hits me I am elsewhere, but the sting overpowers me and I rise.

I walk out to the sitting room with a glare

pushing up against my vision.

Major is already there, standing in the open doorway. I stop where I stand, and there they are, just like Link described. White hoods stop at their neck, and sheets billow over their bodies, but where they hold their torches to the sky, their shirt sleeves are visible. It is clear why she compared them to ghosts, an army of them, but they are real live men. Major is still at the door, facing all of them and I want to run to him, to stand beside him, or behind him, to shield Jericho and Eliza who have come up on the side of me, but I am frozen, gripping the top of the hard-backed chair in front of me like it is what needs protection. Major doesn't look back.

"Lord, deliver me," I say, but no one hears me.

"You got business here with me and my family?" Major asks.

"Lower your voice, boy." One of the men steps out front. His torch is the longest and he aims its fiery point at Major's chest. He has big green eyes, watering through the hood, like he's the one afraid. There are only ten of them, I see now. It seemed like fifty but it is ten.

"You done messed with a good white

282

man's property, and I'm taking you to task for it."

"We apologized for that. We settled with the man himself. He said not to worry about it. Why are you?"

It is like another man has swooped inside of Major. There is laughter from the group. I want to run to my son, tell him to apologize again, whatever he does to drop that knife from inside his throat that is casting his words out so sharp, but I can't move yet.

"You think you can just settle things with a white man, boy? That's what you think?"

Major is silent.

"I'm here to tell you you can't. I'm here to tell you you can't make off with a good white man's property without paying." The white man looks back at the ghosts behind him. I look back at them too. There is one in particular who calls my gaze. It is the shoes I notice first, the ones Charlotte's mama said were nice. There might have been a time when they were, but they are over-polished and dusted up now.

That group Charlotte and her husband are in is the Klan.

The men move upon the house in a rush, and I duck, make for Eliza and Jericho. I hear the glass in the windows shattering as I hobble over. Major runs to the back of the house and comes out cradling his daddy's shotgun in one hand, loading the shells inside it with the other. When he gets outside, the men are already out of range, but he racks the gun, pulls its trigger, and pumps it, and I hold Jericho's ears as the shots ring out. I scream for Major to stop; those shots don't signal safety for me, but he keeps on until he can't anymore, and the men don't come back. We sit amid the glass from the busted-out windows for hours, and they don't come back.

Finally we make moves toward sleeping. We all end up in Jericho's room. I give Eliza the bed and huddle on the floor next to my grandson. Major just stands in the hallway. I expect him to object when Jericho asks me to tell him a story about Wildwood, but he doesn't even seem to hear it; I am facing his back, and it seems straighter than I have ever seen it.

JOSEPHINE

1855

A few days after Daddy drew, he started staying out late. There was a group of men who did this, who stole whiskey and drank it from a gray jug in one of the single men's cabins, but Daddy was not one of them, not until now. Mama didn't say anything but I could tell she was not sleeping because every time I woke up I caught her staring back at me, her near-black eyes unflinching.

One day he came in the cabin all loose in his limbs. The sun wasn't up yet, but it was rising. Mama was already lighting the fire, and she turned to him fast, and said, "What's gotten into you?"

"I've been thinking," he said.

"Thinking about what?"

He paused, removing first one shoe, then the other. "Fred said that they have people in the North who are fighting for slaves to be freed. Abolitionists they're called. He said he heard Tom talking about it with his brother when they brought that old fool slave here. They're making progress, Tom said. Tom said it like it was a bad thing, like something he's worried about."

"Progress be slow sometimes," Mama said. Then she sighed. "You can wait all you want but I'm going on that journey," she told him.

"You think you're so brave, Winnie?"

"I am brave."

"You think you're so brave but another word for brave is stupid. You don't think things through. You don't think through how a ten-year-old girl's going to fare out there in the swamps for weeks with no food and no water. You don't think about how her life's going to change if she's caught."

"Don't talk like that. You know it's against the rules to talk like that."

He grabbed her hand. "I'm just saying we got it easy now. A master that lets us call him by name, as much food as we can eat, we can come and go on the weekends, I'm not in the fields, you not either —"

"It's not freedom." She paused. "You said it yourself. Tom or no Tom, he got the power to snap our necks." Then she added even though she didn't need to: "Not everybody is related," and the air between them seemed to wilt.

"I know better than anybody it's not freedom," Daddy said after a while. "You don't have to tell me. But hearing about those abolitionists, I wonder if we going about it the wrong way. Putting ourselves in danger. Putting our daughter in danger. Maybe it's best to wait. Even if I die bound to this plantation, I'm starting to think Josie's going to get out, her children for sure will. You talk so much about the ancestors' spirits inside us. Then won't her reaching elsewhere be the same as us getting there ourselves?"

Meanwhile Jupiter just wouldn't quit. When I got home the next evening he was there, and he had been there for some time, I could see because his cup of tea was almost empty. Mama got up to refill it.

"You're not going to get far going with him. You know it, I know it," he said. He hadn't even seen me come in, but Mama said with a nod in the other direction, "Go play." I hustled into a corner. I had dolls that Miss Sally gave me and I pretended they were talking to each other. They were saying things like, "Would you like some jam with your bread?" and "What a pretty dress you're wearing today!" But they were thinking, *Who is this man in my house? What can I do to get him out?*

"He pulled twice," Mama said. "Spirit must want him to go if he pulled twice."

"Could just be a coincidence. They say he lucky."

"I don't believe in coincidences. The spirits want him to go if he pulled twice."

Jupiter stood up, then leaned over Mama's shoulder. "Take me with you," he whispered like he suddenly realized somebody else was in the room.

"And leave Domingo? You must be out your mind."

"I didn't say leave Domingo. Calm down, woman; instead of talking, listen sometimes. I didn't say leave Domingo," he repeated. "The three of us could go."

"You mean four?" She jutted her head in my direction, and I grimaced.

"Of course four," he said. "Just didn't count her 'cause she's a child, that's all."

"Nobody's coming between me and my family," Mama said.

He was smirking now, looking her up and down like he knew what was under her wide-swinging skirt and drawn-in blouse. "You don't trust me, do you?"

She raised her eyebrow.

"You don't remember how I handled ol'

Fred. He happier for you than he is for himself. And it's not just Fred, it's all of them who was willing to go against you. Not just them either. I'm reaching my point of maturity. The older I get, the better I am," he said. "I done got so good I could change the thoughts in white people heads too. You remember them diamond earrings? People asked me how I knew where they were. But I didn't. I just changed her mind about it. Whether they were there or not, I made her believe they were. And then she found them."

"Why you didn't get her to think she had already whipped you then?" I asked from where I stood across the room.

He turned toward me and smiled, an eerie pucker of his lips, then he reached for the door handle and looked back toward my mama.

"You think on that. You imagine ol' Domingo in front of a slave catcher and you think about him bumbling and carrying on. Then you imagine me."

When he was gone, Mama walked over and tried to hug me, but I pushed her away. That night, when Miss Sally invited me to stay the night I didn't tell her Mama wanted to sleep with me like normal. I said okay, and I sprawled out on the floor beneath the foot of her bed like I imagined sisters would.

"Josephine?" she asked. "Could you come up here with me just for tonight? It's awful cold, and I hate sleeping alone."

I climbed in. It was almost as good as sleeping next to Mama, and I thought about her sliding into the empty pallet, Daddy still observing Tom's late dinner. She would be missing me, that was for certain, and it filled me up almost to the point of shame.

Miss Sally squeezed me, and I squeezed her back.

"Can I tell you something?" she asked.

I nodded. She moved her hand under her pillow and pulled something out. It was the coin.

"I sleep with it every night. For safety."

I grinned. "That's so nice," I said. "I sleep with mine too. I thought it was just me."

"I need all the protection I can get," she laughed. Then she quieted and said, "Also it reminds me of us and how we're like sisters and I notice I haven't had a bad dream once since I started." She paused. "Mama says you're the devil. Mama says you and your mama are that way, that it ain't natural for a human to have so much power. She told me to stay away from you." She whispered the next part. "But I won't, I can't and I won't."

290

"Thank you, Miss Sally, that's real nice," I said. But I was scared all of a sudden knowing I was breaking a rule I didn't even know existed.

"But what do you want?" she asked.

"What do I want from what?"

"You always grant my wishes with your mind magic, but what do you want for yourself?"

I shrugged. "I'm happy enough," I said because I was, and also because I remembered what Mama said, that for everything a white person gave you they were going to take five things from you in return, and right now Miss Sally had given me peace when I was angry, security when I was afraid, and I wondered how she would get those things back. They were inside of me. Could she reach into my heart and grab them?

"You can tell me," she said. "Your most secret wish."

I shook my head.

"Is it a boy?" she asked.

I shook my head again, giggled some.

"Is it more candy? Is it dresses?"

I shook my head still. "We want to be free," I said, regretting it as soon as it was out, but she only laughed.

"Oh, Josephine, are you serious?" she asked. "You mustn't say such things. You're lucky you said it to me and not someone else; they might not understand your humor" — she paused — "or how naïve you can be."

I nodded. "I'm sorry," I said.

"It's okay, but I just want you to promise to never repeat that again."

I nodded. "I promise."

"Besides, what would I do if you left me, Josephine? I wouldn't have a life fit to live if you weren't here."

I nodded again. I was angry that she laughed at me, but I was relieved too. I'd be forlorn without her and it was nice that she felt the same way. I thought of Mama. She was right and she was also wrong.

The Monday of the week we planned to leave Wildwood, Mama found me in the kitchen cleaning up after Miss Sally's breakfast and dragged me out to an oak tree just beyond the last rows of cane.

"I talked to your daddy yesterday while you were out," she said.

"Um-hmm."

"We thought a lot about it," she hesitated, "and we agree that we have a better chance if Jupiter comes with us."

"That sneak," I shouted.

"Shh." She gripped my wrist. People were

looking over.

"It's just for that reason," she whispered. "Imagine if we get caught on the way. Jupiter can make a white man think we got a pass. Think we supposed to be somewhere we not. Imagine how much power that is."

I shook my head.

"Daddy never would have agreed to that," I said. "Jupiter probably got in his head too, same way he got in everybody else's. You're not afraid he's going to get in yours, Mama?"

"He can't get in mine. I'm more powerful than he is," she said real fast but it was too fast.

Meanwhile we continued to prepare. There were the weekly meetings that turned daily, and every time you saw a Revisioner, whether they were plaiting a baby's hair or stirring porridge, carting stalks of cane to be ground, their mind should have been on the fast and safe departure of the few who were chosen to lead the way. Not only that, there was the carriage that Fred needed to prepare for our journey, the firearms to steal, the meal bags to pack, the other horses whose shoes needed to be damaged so no one could follow us straight away. There was the tripling down of duties so that nobody noticed the four of us had gone until we were long past where the dogs could smell us.

Three days before we were set to leave, Jupiter knocked on the door. "It's time."

"Later," Daddy said. "Everything set for later."

"You ain't heard? Things changed," Jupiter said. "Tom's brother's here. They gon' be drinking all night long. Won't know who gone where how."

I saw Daddy thinking on it like he wanted to resist but he couldn't object to the facts.

"If you coming, now's the time. Safest time. Think about your daughter." Jupiter nodded at me.

And Daddy stood and closed the door. I didn't know what he was thinking but that night just when I was on the verge of sleep, I heard him from the porch singing out in a sweet voice,

By the grace of God I'll meet you,
By the grace of God I'll meet you,
By the grace of God I'll meet you,
On Canaan's happy shore.

Then he lifted me and carried me outside, into the carriage where Mama and Jupiter were waiting. I turned around and stared at

Wildwood long as I could. It was already dark, but I knew it by heart and I counted out goodbyes to each cabin frame, clutching my mama's fingers beside me.

"Ain't nothing here for us now," Mama whispered.

I nodded. I didn't mention Miss Sally, knew Mama wouldn't like it, and my heart was so tender it would break under the weight of leaving her. I firmed it up instead with anger.

"I hate it here. I hate everybody on this here place. Missus, especially."

Mama paused for a minute before she answered me. Her eyes were closed and I thought she might be issuing her own private prayer. "I done told you about hate," she said. "What do we believe in?" she asked.

"God," I said back without needing to think. "Our own immortal souls. The ancestor spirit," I added.

"And what happens to the ancestor spirit when it dies?"

"It comes back into my children, their children, their children's children."

She paused again, let me consider what I'd said. "You ever think about what it will come back to?" she asked.

"No, ma'am," I said back.

"Well, you think about it, because it's up to you. The ancestors come back with whatever heart they left behind. If it's a hateful one, they come back hating. Whoever they hated come right back with them, in one form or another."

I didn't know what she was talking about. It was late, and all I wanted was my old mat on the floor, my mama on one side of me and my daddy on the other.

"It's not possible to do anything but hate certain people," Jupiter said, and he lifted the whip to hurry the mule. The pigeon was sleeping in his lap.

I found myself agreeing with him for once but I was too tired to speak on it.

"It's possible," Mama said back. "You just think about how much they must be rotting deep down inside. And you remember, what you can't love, you see again. It's not just this life either."

AVA

The day after Grandma calls me a thief, there is nowhere to go but to my mother's.

I start talking as soon as she opens the door. I tell her about Grandma, about her comments, how they've been ramping up, and about last night, how she accused me of taking something she had given me. It had meant so much to me that she had given it to me, and then she took it all back.

"I can't be in the house with her anymore," I say. "I'm going out of my mind, truly, but then I wonder if I'm being selfish. She's obviously going through something, dementia or Alzheimer's, hell I don't know what. But it's not just that. The things she says, Mama. Terrible things. Sometimes it takes me a while to figure out how terrible they are. And the tone. I know she's my grandmother but I didn't grow up with her. Sometimes I look at her, and I just see a

297

white lady treating me like a —"

"I believe it," my mother says.

"You saw it the first time you came over, and I didn't listen." I shake my head. "What's wrong with me that I didn't? What was blinding me? And then I exposed King to it."

We are still standing in the entryway. I can hear the kettle signal the water is ready for the tea and she motions for me to follow her to the kitchen. I watch her pour a cup, then fish around her cabinet for a saucer. She hands both to me, and I take a sip.

"Don't blame yourself," she says. "That's what they want you to do, turn all their hate inward so the focus is off their bad behavior. Remember too, I'm older than you are. When I met Martha, she was in her prime. I loved your daddy so much, and more than anything, I wanted her to accept me. She pretended to, but she never did, not fully. When she introduced me to people, she'd say I was your daddy's wife, never her daughter-in-law. She'd ask me to take pictures of her, her husband, and your daddy like I wasn't a part of the family. And maybe I wasn't." My mother shakes her head. "Maybe I wasn't. And like you say, it was the way she talked to me. She grew up with black folks waiting on her hand and foot. She could have fought harder to get that dynamic out of her system, but she didn't. She preferred to pretend it wasn't there. I'm not saying she didn't get better. She did; I think having you as a grandchild was the best thing that could have happened to her. It changed the culture of that family, no doubt, but under the surface, the old ways were still brewing."

"And now it's coming out," I say.

"And now it's coming out," she says.

Having someone agree with me calms me down. I start to remember how the old woman fell onto my shoulder that morning, and my guilt rises.

"Maybe I'm exaggerating," I say. "She's my grandmother and she's sick. Maybe I'm taking it all too personal. She's losing her mind, and she's done so much for me; maybe now is the time to stay and pay her back."

"Stop that." The words jut out so sharp I expect there to be a pop on my hand the way there used to be in childhood if I answered back *What* instead of *Yes, ma'am,* if I had the nerve to talk to my mother like she was my little friend.

"When you were a little girl, you wanted your daddy so bad. Every night, you'd ask me if he was coming back. I knew one day something like this would trip you up. You would always ask me why that side didn't invite you to their functions. You would always fantasize about what was going on between those walls. It makes sense that you needed to see for yourself."

"It's too bad what happened to Martha," she goes on. "I hate that she's sick, trust me I do. But everything you got" — she pokes me in the chest — "you earned it, girl." She taps me with each word. "She didn't give you a thing another grandmother wouldn't have given you ten times as much of. You gave her respect, that's all you owed her, but your peace, you deserve that, and you can't let nobody take it away from you."

I stick around my mother's house for another hour after that. She has errands to run, but it is hard going back to Martha's, nearly impossible. When I do go, I walk in to the sound of her talking. I can hear the end of her conversation with Binh. She is complimenting him on the wheat bread he bought from the farmer's market. It tastes better than Whole Foods'. She doesn't know why it took her so long to figure that out. I can tell that she's in her right mind. Accusing me of stealing was my limit though, and I don't have a month in me. I'm not ready to buy my own place, but I'll stay with my mother in the meantime. Now I just need to tell Martha.

I sit down next to her and she lights up at my face. This is the woman I know, the woman I had adored. She's eating yogurt and granola, a tiny portion of it, and with each bite she closes her eyes as if to stretch the flavor.

"You know, I only wanted to get on my feet," I start, "to help you as long as I could, but it's been three months now." I pause.

Her face slackens.

"Three months is a long time to be in somebody else's space." It's taking everything in me to keep going. "I'm grown," I go on. "King and I are a family, and we need to start this next chapter on our own."

She doesn't look at me while I'm talking, and when I'm done, she pushes the bowl away.

"You're abandoning me?" she asks, but she doesn't say it in a dramatic way. She might as well have asked me if I wanted the rest of the yogurt.

"No, I'm not abandoning you," I say.

"I'm just kidding," she says back, and her face lights up again, too fast though, maybe too fast. "I'm just kidding," she repeats. "I understand. You're young, you have King, you don't want to be bogged down with some old biddy. I understand better than anybody," she goes on. "I left home when I was seventeen, was married at twenty. My mother would call me the Lone Wolf. You must have gotten that from me. When are you headed out?"

"I don't know exactly," I say. I hear my voice deepening. "Actually I'm thinking about tonight." I hold my head up when I say it.

"You won't have time to find a place that soon."

"No, but I'll stay with my mother while I'm looking."

Her face darkens again then, but she is still sounding upbeat, trying to. "Yes, that makes sense with all the work you've been doing together." Each word is like a tiptoe, a ballerina's sequence of jumps. "King will stay at the school," she continues. "It's not that far of a drive. You can get anywhere within the city of New Orleans in fifteen minutes, that's what people don't realize." And then she lets out a cold sliver of a laugh.

"I guess I'll be getting on then," she says. And she stands up unassisted. I start to help to see her off, but she seems fine and I sit back down.

I pack. First King's room, then mine, and

in a couple of hours, I've made headway. Like I said, there isn't much, clothes and rugs and my great-great-great-grandmother's picture. I look at it now and it appears that she's smiling; it appears, without me trying too hard to decipher what I want to see, that she's proud. There's the lamp that Martha bought from Nordstrom to replace the one that she chipped, and it's beautiful, eerily similar, but I think I'll leave it here. As if to express her discontent, I hear a sniffle behind me.

"The Dufrene girls," she starts.

"Now, Martha, that's enough."

"Not just to the white boys," she goes on, and I turn. She has entered the room and opened the top drawer of my dresser, rooting through it, not even looking at me while she speaks.

"There were black ones too, who would look, glance in my direction. They barely had the gall to smile but I made them know what my intentions were. I did. And one night, I convinced one to come over. I gave him the night of his life. One he'll always remember." She's still rummaging through the drawers. I'm not sure what she's looking for but I've never heard this new version of her story and I can't help but pay close attention.

"But I'm afraid," she goes on. "I'm afraid it might not have been enough. My brothers took after my father's side. They always wanted to hear Great-Granddaddy's stories. The cotton, the dances, the parties Great-Great-Grandmother would throw for the slaves at Wildwood. It didn't sicken my brothers the way it did me, and when I saw what they did to that boy, well, I begged them to turn themselves in, but I was the baby of the family. The youngest girl. The prettiest girl in the entire county."

Now she's at the drawer where I keep my money. She's opened it, removed a wad of folded $100 bills. I step toward her and try to wrestle them from her hand, but it's too late. She straightens a few out, then rips them into shreds.

I reach for the rest of the pile in the drawer and she blocks me with one hand, holding on to the dresser with the other. She is still in her nightgown, pale blue with lace at the fringes, and it sways in the scuffle. Her hand on the dresser is red from her tight grip. Her other hand is slapping me, but I hold it back and reach for the remaining bills. She gives up fighting and starts screaming.

"That's not yours. You didn't earn it. I paid you that money to stay with me. I didn't give you that money to leave. Don't touch me," she yells. "Don't you touch me," and she holds down the button on her monitor.

I hear the operator answer.

"Nine-one-one, what's your emergency?"

She pauses just for a second, and I rip the monitor from her hand. She's too taken aback to fight me.

"It's my grandmother," I say. "She needs help. She's having some sort of mental break, and she needs help."

She seems to deflate when I say those words. All the effort she had exerted in the last few minutes has worn her out and she places her hand on the dresser to hold herself upright.

While the operator asks me questions, Martha watches me with a curious expression, her head cocked to one side. When I hang up, she slumps onto the floor, but I don't go to lift her. I walk downstairs and wait.

I hear the ambulance approach, and as soon as the paramedics ring the bell, I open the door and let them in. When they've found her, I take my suitcase to the car first, then King's, then the decorations and appliances I've carried. The picture is last. I carry it with me the way I used to carry

King when he was a baby. I don't need to look at Josephine's face to know what she's feeling, what she's thinking even: *Don't look back.* The whole while I walk, Martha's still screaming.

"You're never going to get away from me, you're never going to make it out there in the world. You're never going to make it, leaving me."

They have carried her out onto the stretcher now.

"You're never going to be nothing." I can hear her until I open the car door, then close it. I'm tempted to look back at the sirens, even at her, but I fix my gaze forward.

JOSEPHINE

1924

The next morning I set to baking my best bread. It is not the ordinary loaf. I drop walnuts in the batter, a pinch of cinnamon too. I slice ginger and sprinkle it in; I've seen a loaf of it straight from the oven make a grown man cry.

When it has risen, I wrap it in cloth and walk next door. I can hear noise from inside, and I almost don't raise my fist. It is clear Charlotte has company, but my nerves have been grinding on me all morning, and I can't sit with them alone another minute.

She opens the door and her face falls. She thought it was somebody else, or she isn't in a position to entertain me, I can't make out which, but she does not want me there. And I didn't want to come. I am angry, knowing what I now know about her, apprehensive too, standing there, but there isn't much I wouldn't do to secure peace;

there isn't anything I wouldn't do to protect my son. I extend my arm.

"Made you some bread," I say. "It was my turn." I giggle the way I've heard her do. It is my first time and it doesn't come out quite right. I can hear that it is more like a pig's grunt than anything.

Anyway.

"It will go mighty nice with any jam you've got stored."

"Oh, that's so kind of you." Her smile is back and I'm glad I tarried. She takes the bread from me. "I'm in the middle of something though," she says.

"Oh? I didn't mean to interrupt. I just wanted to talk to you." I pause. "It's important actually." I hear the voices rising behind her.

"Oh? Oh," she says. "Look, I know there's something going on between you and Vern with that godawful tree. I hated that tree anyway." She waves her hand. "Between you and me I'm glad it's gone." She is wearing lipstick. Blush too. And her hair is pulled back in a bun. She is a beautiful woman. All this time I didn't know it. "Either way I think it should stay between the men, don't you?"

I don't know what to say. It is not a hard question, but the way she has asked it, the way she stands with her shoulders back — and she has big breasts, enormous ones. Mine have never been so large, not even when I was carrying children, and I don't know how I missed that on her — makes me falter.

"I was thinking maybe we could work something out though, Miss Charlotte," I say. "Of course it's often wise to let business matters stay where they belong but this time because we have a relationship, because it's such a sensitive issue to both sides, I thought maybe we could clear it out on this end."

"I'd rather not discuss it now either way," she says, and the door starts to swing in my direction.

I put my foot between it and the slot.

"My son is under a lot of pressure is the thing and I know if we just got together and talked the way we used to, we could smooth this out for both our guys. Ease the weight on their shoulders a bit," I go on.

There is a shriek from behind her, and she looks back.

"Okay, let's talk about it another time. I've really got to get back to them."

The door edges forward, this time almost to my face.

"Okay, maybe later today?" I ask, my foot

out farther to block the door from closing.

"Maybe," she says, and a woman walks up behind her.

"You okay out here, Charlotte? You need help with something?" She walks closer.

"No, I was just on my way back." Charlotte waves her hand behind her to keep her friend from tracking forward, but the movement only catches the other woman's attention and draws her out.

"You sure, Charlotte? You've been gone a mighty long time, and with a room full of guests. Margaret was looking for the plates and couldn't find them. I tried to search your cabinets but they are full of dust. Don't you have a girl? If not, I have a recommendation." She reaches the parlor and sees my face. "Oh." She steps back. "Is this one bothering you, Charlotte?" she asks.

"No, no." Charlotte pushes the door back and I barely move my foot in time. I hear her through the wood. "She was just begging is all."

"Those people. Well that's what our work is all about," her friend says, and then their voices trail off. I turn around and look back over the fields that Isaiah mastered. Normally I feel majestic beholding it all, but today it is like it belongs to someone else, and I am on Wildwood again standing

beyond the missus' table, waiting for Miss
Sally to finish eating so I can devour her
scraps.

The big day is growing closer so I start to sleep at Major's house. He has to help Eliza put her shoes on these days. She takes all her meals in the bed, and she's dropped so when the baby kicks she has to call for a bucket. Since the night those boys busted up their windows, she and Major are getting along better than ever.

"Can I rub your feet, sweetie?" he'll ask.

And she'll reply, all "Thank you so much, my king."

She is proud of him is the thing and I see how that fattens him up on the inside. He is walking around cracking jokes and singing, and I wonder if Eliza's brother wasn't right. The men haven't been back. They had their say and Major had his, and it was harmless in the long run, but it has meant so much to Major to feel like a man.

When I do go back home for fresh clothes, I make sure it is light out. It is Klan country now and I don't want to be caught out after dark.

I pack some blouses for myself. I'd been wearing Eliza's pregnancy skirts, taking out the waistlines on her regular pants just as much for myself as for her. I am in the middle of folding my panties when I hear the knock. I assume it is Theron and open the door, but no. It is Charlotte staring back at me.

She is all marked, much worse than the first time, around both eyes and her mouth. There are rings of bruises around her neck. I gasp and, when my hand leaves the frame of the door, she walks in.

"I tried to tell him to stop, that night," she says. "I wanted to tell you that when you came over, but the other ladies were there. That night you came, I brought it up again, after all the ladies left, and he did this." She gestures over her body. "Told me to mind my own business. I'm so sorry about it, all of it. I told him to stop but he beat me for it, beat me worse than he ever has done. I hadn't told him but I was pregnant that time."

"Still?" I ask.

She shakes her head. "I lost it that night. Maybe I was going to lose it anyway." She looks away at the window.

313

"I'm sorry about that," I say. "Nobody deserves that."

There is silence then. I can tell she expects more from me, applause maybe for what she has given up, taken on my behalf.

"Well, I just came to apologize. I know you don't think much of me now, but I couldn't live with myself if I didn't explain it to you. I'm better than Vern, I'm better than what he did, and I just wanted to make sure I told you that."

She turns to walk away and I almost let her go, but there is a feeling in my chest like the urge to bear down and push, and it is impossible to let it pass.

"That group you joined, that was the Klan, huh?" I ask.

She turns back, nods slowly.

She starts to say more, and I hold up my hand. I walk to the door and hold it open for her. "You ought to leave him," I say.

And she looks down at her shoes again and she walks out.

I start out for the tree where I pray, and the reasons I had been before stretch themselves out before me like a bridge leading me to the exact spot where the grass stopped growing the year my daughter left. Sometimes I would come to just sit and as soon as I'd shut my eyes, it would feel like a plug was stretching from the crown of my head to the great world beyond. Angels would drift over me laughing in my ear. But that wasn't all. There were the times I'd rush over heaving, and I'd swing and I'd punch and I'd scream it all out, all the indignities of being born black and a woman, and my cries would be met with pure silence, but my walk back would feel like floating on the top sheen of a river; my chest would feel like an empty channel. Now I don't know what will come. I close my eyes, and the woman meets me right where I am. The one I see from time to time in my visions, and she is sitting across from me at a great table, a table that stretches near the length of the room. I look all around me and don't recognize a thing, not the wood masks on the wall or the crystal vase almost blocking my view. The woman is beyond my imagination with her nails and teeth glistening and her hair in long gray knots, wrapped at the top with a scarf. She smiles at me.

"I've been waiting on you to come, and show yourself to me," she says.

"Who are you?" I ask her.

"Who are you?" she asks, almost like an echo, and I look up at her then because of the charm of her words, like a smooth rock being cradled all around in someone's hands, and she catches me and smiles again. "I am you, and you are me, so whoever you are, that's who I am too." And she laughs for a long stretch of time. "I've been waiting for you," she says again.

I look around some more. The room, everything in it, is so polished. So new. There are photographs on every surface and rugs that snap your attention in oranges and golds. There's a large square in the center of the room with moving pictures of people flashing across it. Reminds me of the shows people talked about in New Orleans, but in her own home. I want to touch it, but I still have the manners my mother molded into me.

"You been waiting on me?" I ask.

She nods again. "Every day. I've been watching you too. Seeing what you're up to. You were a slave, weren't you?"

I raise my head. "More like they were enslavers, girl. We would have done anything to change things," I say. "But that was just the way they were. Even still, my parents risked their lives. And nothing was the same after that."

As I speak, it is hard to ignore her clothes. Eliza couldn't even imagine the silk, the way the shirt accentuates the breasts just so, and the sharp cut of the skirt. And she says she's me. All this time, Mama was right.

"I'm proud of you," I say.

She starts to smile but then her mouth closes up, her right eye waters. "Of me?" she asks. "Are you serious?"

She stands, walks over to me; the closer she comes, the more I can smell her, the waft rising in my nostrils with every step. I don't know if it's flowers or hot vanilla; it is as fancy as Missus' rose water was, but it smells good.

I push my chair toward her. She holds her hands out to me, and I accept them.

"I couldn't be more proud of *you,*" she says. "We couldn't repay it. We just couldn't repay it all."

She reaches out to hug me but a voice juts in from beyond our table. I can't see who it belongs to, but I hear it call to her, "Gladys." She looks back, and I open my eyes.

JOSEPHINE

1855

I drifted off to sleep, and when I woke, Jupiter was yelling to get out of the carriage. We stood at the edge of marshes and reeds that reached my shoulders. Daddy bent down to lift me, and we waded through the swamps for some time. Along the way, Jupiter slapped the water with sticks to ward off moccasin snakes and alligators, and Mama prayed under her breath. When we reached a patch of dry land, we climbed on top of it and felt the ground beneath us crackle, interwoven palm reeds and leaves. Four men leapt from nowhere we could see. They wore tattered cotton pants and shirts, and hats and coats made from raccoon skins. They each held a gun to Jupiter's chest.

"The shining man sent us," Jupiter said, and the men nodded and grunted, then dropped their guns to their sides, and motioned for us to follow. We hadn't gone far before we came upon a row of huts lifted on stilts.

"Where are they taking us?" my mama asked, and Daddy shushed her. We climbed up a ladder and followed the men to the cabin farthest off. The door was open, and newspapers sealed the walls, with blankets covering pallets of grass. There was a fire going, and we drifted toward the heat. A man a smooth shade of brown with straight gray hair to his shoulders sat with his legs folded. There was no question he was the shining one, not only because his face gleamed like someone had just slathered it in lard but because of the way the other men shifted around him, bowing when they walked in, and as fierce as they had seemed to us, their voices here lowered and softened. When the shining man saw Jupiter, he sang a tune I'd heard before.

Ma lo we l'okun mo

It took me some time to recognize the source but then it came to me. It was that same song Jupiter sang when he saw Mama. Jupiter and my mama looked at each other, and when the shining man finished, they sang a different verse right back at him.

Mama had dressed me in everything I owned but I was wet from the walk over, and I stood there shivering. The shining man directed my mother to cover me and he passed me a tin cup of water. I drank while they spoke. I was more tired than I had ever been before and while I slept, scraps of their conversation wove together like the branches that formed the walls around me.

They hadn't expected a child, the shining man said.

They didn't have children here, on account of what they were made to do.

"We're not staying long," my mother said, but she was shushed again, this time by Jupiter.

"She's not like a normal child," he said. "She's quicker than most adults. She can mind herself. She can work."

"We don't allow children here," the shining man repeated, as if they hadn't even spoken.

My mother started to cry.

"Just for a few days, then," my daddy said. "Just a few days and we'll be on our way."

The shining man seemed to consider that for a minute, then he nodded and said we could sleep in the cabin next to his. Daddy lifted me again and carried me over to it. There were two mats inside, and a pail of water, but no one drank from it. Jupiter collapsed onto one of the mats, and my parents did the same on another. I slept between them and as scared as I knew I should be, I felt safe.

There was no bell to wake us but we woke at dawn just the same. Outside, some men were frying rabbit over a fire and they set chunks of meat on a tin plate for us. Jupiter devoured his but my daddy only had a bite. He gave the rest to my mother and me. It was tough, and as hungry as I was, I had to chew each bite so long I grew tired of eating.

After that, we all went to work. The women tended their gardens of corn and squash, and the men ventured into the woods to cut trees or to hunt. I helped my mother spread seeds and rip weeds out, but there were twenty women there, and there was only so much to do. After lunch, we all gathered again in a circle. The prayers started out just like they had at Wildwood, gratitude for free air to breathe, a soft place to lay our heads in the night. And then Mama started chanting a song I hadn't

heard before, the men and the women surrounding her joining in:

No more peck o' corn for me
No more peck o' corn for me
No more peck o' corn for me
Many thousand go

They lifted their voices and clapped their
hands. Some stomped their feet and swung
in a circle. There were drums and rattles
here, and people took turns playing and
shaking them, their mouths to the sky.

No more mistress' call for me
No more mistress' call for me
No more mistress' call for me
Many thousand go

When it was over, I was able to walk
around the camp. It was true that there were
no other children. Mostly the men clung to
one side, and the women clung to the other,
but there was separation outside of that too.
Jupiter traveled with the men who met us
with guns and Daddy sat in silence with the
shining man. I followed Jupiter. There were
many trees in my path, mostly oak and yellow pine. Small cattle abounded, dashing
away from me in wild spurts as I ap-
proached. I came to a creek a few yards

from our cabin, where Jupiter and his crew of men sat fishing. I stayed far enough back that they couldn't smell me or hear me breathing. They didn't say much at first, just watched for the top of the water to ripple but after a while they started sharing stories about where they had come from, where they hoped to go.

At first he thought he'd run alone, to Ohio, then Canada, Jupiter said. He knew people who had done it. No, they hadn't gotten word to him, but he could feel in his spirit that they had reached the North. They were that close to him, and he had planned it out so that he would do the same. Then he met this woman.

The other men grunted.

Not like that, he said. He wouldn't risk his life for that. It was more like she was his home, what it would feel like if he had ever known it, a far-off memory of what it could have been. And he had a responsibility to help her. If not her, her child.

It soothed me to hear him talk like that, but the men weren't impressed.

That sounded nice, they said. Real nice, they repeated. But every week someone went back to the plantation for supplies. The thing was, when new people came, they took priority. Which one was it going to be?

I expected Jupiter to offer up my daddy, that was the kind of man I had known him to be, but he said he would go. He smiled real big when he said it, his crazy, wide-eyed, out-of-his-mind smile. And the men patted him on the back and passed him something dark to drink.

Later, after supper, my mother walked up behind him and slapped him on the arm. She took off toward the creek and he followed. I wasn't too far behind them.

"Don't be stupid," I heard her say when I neared her. "We just left the place and you going back."

"It's different now, though. It's my own agency. I'm going back as a free man."

"You ain't free yet, fool. They find you, you be right back on that plantation, but this time with one less ear or leg."

He laughed like he did, head back and full-bodied. "You forget all your Revisioner talk now, huh? What you look like, wondering what's going to become of me. Shouldn't you be envisioning me walking back, not even running because there's nobody on my tail? Shouldn't you be envisioning my arms full of meat, clothes, guns?"

My mama just shook her head.

"Just let me do my work, woman," he said.

"Yeah, you do your work, all right," she

said, "but I'm telling you, whether you back or not, in two days, we leaving for that steamboat."

Daddy walked up then, smiling. He had had some of the dark drink himself.

"What y'all arguing about?" he asked, pulling Mama to him. "Some people can't even enjoy the fruit of their prayers." He kissed her on the mouth.

"Not yet," she said. "Soon though." She slid up to Daddy but she looked back at Jupiter with hate in the corner of her eyes. Or maybe it was fear.

He was gone when I woke up the next morning. We didn't do anything different on account of it. My mother picked weeds from okra and talked to the other ladies about the steamboat leaving for the North on the Mississippi. At night, the men sat around the fire and sharpened their knives and axes and hatchets and built their guns, then took them apart and built them again. They said if the man didn't come back, we could expect the whites to come for us tomorrow. And they agreed they'd spend the night on the path we crossed upon arriving, and wait.

Nobody mentioned Jupiter's name, and I hadn't liked him, but it didn't feel right, that if he went, these people wouldn't have been touched by him. My mama though was wringing her hands out like they were rags. She was pacing, and my daddy walked up behind her and told her to *calm down, woman,* and then the second time, he said, "You making us all nervous over here, calm down." But it didn't make a difference, and by the time I settled in for bed, I assumed Jupiter was gone.

Sometime after I went to sleep but before the sun rose, I heard a gunshot. I sat straight up and Mama let out a long bending wail. We hurried outside the cabin, my daddy holding Mama up, and there Jupiter was, standing right in front of us, the pigeon on his shoulder. He was laughing with the men, carrying even more guns, a chicken, shirts, some wool pants, and four pairs of leather boots. My mother didn't approach him, she just stood right next to me shaking her head and smiling. We went back inside to bed, but my father didn't come back to sleep with us. He stood by the door until I fell asleep and when Mama and I woke, he was still there, standing.

Mama looked up at him and sighed.

She got up and took out the bowl and the wooden spoon the other women had given us and she cracked three eggs and began to whip them. Like he had asked a question, she spoke.

"It's not like that." She dragged more than walked to a small barrel and began sifting corn flour for bread. "He's like a brother," she went on. "You never had a brother, so you don't know. When I talk to him I feel like I'm in my mama's arms. I can barely remember it. I couldn't pick out her face in a crowd, but I remember the feeling I'd have, and it is pure."

Daddy didn't say anything. He moved in close to her and watched her fry bread over the skillet fire. Several times he'd open his mouth but then he'd close it again and when the bread was ready he ate every bite.

We fell into a routine: gardening, cleaning, bathing, cooking, sitting with the men while they described their wives, the women they wanted to be their wives. During certain parts, Mama would lean over to me and cover my ears with her hard, peeling hands. Jupiter and my mama and daddy would talk about freedom, how it would taste, look, and sound, and that's when the rest of the group would go quiet. Daddy asked them if they wanted to join us, and they shook their heads.

Some of them said it wasn't worth it; some of them said they were happy where they were; one said his work started and ended here, that this was the part that called him. It wouldn't work as well for us if they weren't here, another one echoed. One day, maybe, they'd leave, but for now, they had to see people like us through.

The women knew the details about the steamboat, that it left New Orleans just when the sun was coming up, that we'd sneak on board, that we'd hide in the cargo for as many nights as it took to reach Cincinnati. I had gotten used to the camp though, even to the men with guns. More than that, I didn't want to give up sleeping between my mama and daddy. I didn't dare say it but I had even imagined staying there forever, and when I got older, sneaking off with Jupiter to pilfer some nights. I could say hi to Miss Sally. She was a heavy sleeper and she wouldn't know me from a dream.

The goodbyes the next night were hard and fast. The women passed us okra and greens, corn bread and fish and the men handed Jupiter a gun and my daddy a hatchet. It was a thirty-mile walk to the boat. The Mississippi River coursed by beside us, hemmed in by the levee we'd snuck across so many nights. Oaks and orange trees stood on the other side, plantations raised up behind them, distinct from Wildwood, but I could trace their outlines by what I knew. There would be the cabins, there would be the sugar mill, there would be the kitchen, there would be the fields, there would be the big house lording above it all. Most of the walk was flat land, but there were ditches too. When there weren't wooden bridges to cross them, Mama and the men waded through water to their waists, and Daddy carried me on his shoulders.

We had been walking for most of the night before we stopped for water. I was kneeling beside the river when I heard a man's voice behind us.

I didn't need to turn around to know he was white.

"Where do you think you're going?" he asked.

We didn't move or answer.

"Where do you think you're going?" he asked again.

This time, Jupiter turned and we all turned with him.

I could see the man startle when he saw Jupiter's face.

"We're just going for a walk," Jupiter said. "Looking for a man to buy a gun from. You know anybody?"

My daddy's grip on my hand tightened. I could feel him reach beneath his coat for his hatchet. My mother stood right behind me but I couldn't feel her breathing. I had stopped breathing myself in that small moment. I didn't understand why Jupiter would be so stupid. But the white man didn't flinch.

"No, sir," he said. "But the closer you get to New Orleans, the more likely you'll be to find what you're looking for."

"That's what we were thinking," Jupiter said. "Well, we might as well be on our way then."

"You have a good day, sir, you hear?" the white man said, and Jupiter lifted his hat, and bid him good day too.

When the man was out of sight, Daddy and Mama looked at each other in disbelief. Jupiter nodded, patting them on the backs. "I told you so," he said more than once.

"You're right, you did," Daddy said back. "But if it hadn't worked —" he started.

"But it did," Jupiter said.

"It did," Mama repeated.

And we started to walk again, faster this time, spurred on by the threat behind us, though it had passed.

By sunup we could glimpse the masts of the ships in the distance but we'd need another night to reach the dock so we made a camp where we stood. We ate vegetables the women had yanked out of the ground for my mother. There were raccoons and possums but Daddy said we shouldn't start a fire. My daddy and Jupiter sat up talking. Mama carried stones with her and she'd shake them in her hands and toss them on the dirt, frown, scoop them up, and toss them down again. She did that three times before she clasped her hands together and closed her eyes. I couldn't hear her prayer, only that the words ran together in a frightened plea.

JOSEPHINE

1924

The bell rings for Eliza that morning, and I can hear her before I reach her house. I know that scream from anywhere, and it calls up my own experience three times over with that winding ache that felt like it would wrench my own life from me. I quicken my pace. There is no time to think once I get there. I am boiling water and moving her between positions and it is the only peace I have had since that first crop was rooted out. Cyrile is there but she doesn't know what to do and she heeds me when I tell her to pile the quilts over the mattress to save the bed and boil the shoestrings to tie the cord and make a salve from cow tallow, to help Eliza to her knees. When the baby is born, and I have placed her in her mother's arms, Cyrile reaches for me, and I hold her while she sobs.

They let Jericho name his sister.

"Lucille," he says.

"That's some pretty, Jericho," I say.

"Where'd you get it?" Major asks.

"Girl from my school."

Major and I look at each other and laugh.

"You gone name my daughter after some girl you got a crush on at school, Jericho James?"

He shrugs.

"It's pretty," Eliza says. The little girl is the same coloring as her mama, but looks like Major. Looks like Isaiah, and I know he's watching.

"Lucille Josephine. Some pretty."

I ask them if they want me to go home. "No harm in it," I say, if they want to start out as a family, but they reassure me they want me there, so I set to work: stewing the gizzards, tying the baby's cord, stitching Eliza, wrapping her tight, changing the pads, washing the quilts. The baby is up every two hours, so I take her in the mornings. New spirits shouldn't leave their own home for six weeks, but I figure I can make an exception for my farm, so I walk her to the fields her grandfather laid out, point out the potatoes, the tomatoes, the corn.

"You look at it from this angle and life is all the way good, baby girl," I tell her. "You look at it from this angle and you can have anything your little heart can dream up. Anything," I repeat, and the lie trips in my throat, but I repeat it anyway because maybe for her it will be true. Doesn't make it any less true because I said it.

And like life is responding to me, saying, *yes, he can make a new thing,* one morning I am laundering at my own house and there's a knock on the door. It is Link. A man stands next to her, and it takes me a full minute to recognize that it is her son, Henry. He is twenty pounds lighter, his cheeks sink in at their tops, and he doesn't look at me full on in the face, but it is him. I wrap my arms around him and hold him to me for a long time.

Back at Major's, Eliza's milk still isn't in, so I ask Jericho to pull fennel from my fields.

"He's doing his homework; I'll go," Major says. He is easier on the boy lately. Since the baby, Jericho has regressed, wanting to sleep at the bottom of my bed, throwing fits over tiny slights, but Major has overlooked it all, and I wonder if it is on account of how he was allowed to speak his mind to white folks without the world splitting; if he is starting to think there's room for his son to have a mind too.

Eliza takes a nap after Major leaves, and when she wakes up he's still not back.

I feed them dinner — no use waiting; the girl has to eat so the baby can eat — and I clear the plates, but still no Major. I am beginning to get nervous, so I go to Link's. Henry is sitting in the living room with her, and she is buoyed up by his new presence.

"Go and stay with Eliza and the baby," she tells me. "I'll get Theron." Another hour passes, though, and they are still gone.

Eliza is fit to be tied now, up pacing the room though I told her to sit down so her stitches won't burst.

Jericho has gone to sleep and I am glad. When he wakes up his daddy will be back, and he won't have known there was reason to worry. I tell Eliza to do the same.

"The baby is sleeping, you sleep. When you get up, he'll be back," I say.

She shakes her head. "I just don't know where else he would go."

"Probably out looking for something nice for you, to surprise you," I say.

"At this hour?" She looks up at me and I don't have the presence of mind to respond. I am frazzled myself.

Finally I hear Link trudge up the stairs.

"Nothing," she says, shaking her head. "Theron is still out there. Maybe he just went for a walk."

"Probably," I say, though none of us believe it now. I am thinking about the way he spoke to that hooded man who walked to the front, the gunshots blazing. The anticipation of new life, the joy of it, might have stunned me. There is no white man that would abide that. How could I have imagined otherwise? Link stands.

"I'm going to go back to my house," she says. "Theron is still out there. He'll turn up."

I nod.

"Try to get some sleep," she says, but it is not a real suggestion. Link has children. She knows I'll be sitting up here as long as it takes.

I grip the arm of the porch chair while I wait.

Link isn't gone more than a minute when I hear her scream. I stand up and Theron is on the other side of the gate.

"We found him on the farm," I hear him tell her. Then he looks up and sees me. "Go back inside," he says. He is walking toward me. Then he is on me, trying to carry me back in, but I push past him. I walk as fast as my old legs can carry me. I can hear Link and Theron behind me. Though I know, I am walking just in case. Just in case Major is at the farm plowing the fields or planting the seeds or uprooting the potatoes or simply observing the land as I have done so many times, in all its might.

As I walk, I am desperate for each moment before I reach Major to stay with me, to wrap me up inside it, to grip me beyond release. But I hurry too. I can't reach him fast enough. I pass the workers' log houses, the cane mill and the cotton gin, my oak tree and my hog pen. I am nearing the garden when I see him.

It takes me some time to understand it is him: his pants are soiled, his head swings sideways, the left side of his face is crushed, his eyes are wild, this baby that I carried inside me, and that I held to my breast, and I can see his most vulnerable moments splayed in front of me. The first time he fell on his head, he looked up at me and cried, the open-faced shock of a boy just learning about disappointment, just learning about hurt, and he had thought that I would keep him from it. And there was that expression again the first time I told him not to look a white man in the eye, but I failed him because I didn't tell him enough, I didn't

337

tell him in a way that would stick to his bones, I didn't repeat it, I didn't. Whatever I didn't do left a hole inside him that needed to be plugged, and this is what it came to, and the cry that leaves my soul is one that will never be quieted, and the agony of it fills me and will never be emptied.

Link and Theron are upon me, trying to lift me from Isaiah's crops. It is the crops' fault too I think, the fault of this farm, and I rip them out one by one, every single row I can touch, and when I am too tired to keep ripping, I collapse again, and I know Theron and Link are there though I can't feel a thing.

The bell rings, for me this time, for my boy, and I remember Jericho. I stand up and walk. He must never see this. Just the chance that he might step outside and follow his instinct to this spot moves me forward. When I reach the house, Eliza is at the door with the baby, waiting for something good, and I want to be able to give it to her, but just the sight of me wrecks her. She falls down in the doorway, and Link goes for Lucille before she drops. Jericho is by the door, and I hurry over to him, I take him in my arms. I start to tell him what has happened, but he refuses me, shakes his head, rips himself from my arms, covers his ears.

Link walks up to me, the baby in her arms. "We're going to get through this," she says. But we won't. Not me, not now. I wonder about that woman though, the one with the long gray hair who has a child. I try her, back inside myself. She is there; so is her daughter; a boy is with them too. She is sitting with them all, and maybe they are waiting for me.

JOSEPHINE

Whatever danger Mama had glimpsed in the stones that morning seemed to have passed by night. She was in a good mood, joking about the white man we'd encountered, covering our path to the harbor with admonitions.

"You can make a tea out of sassafras or hen feathers, Josie. Castor oil for bowel movements. Animal fat for a salve. Those stones I toss, nothing special about them. Pick them off the ground and smooth them, burn sage and say a prayer, make them holy. Anything you can touch, you can make holy."

When she finished, we went over our plan. Jupiter still carried the clothes he'd stolen from the plantation, and when we reached the city, we were to wash ourselves in the river and change into them, walk through the central square like the free people we were born to be, like the free people we were now. There was a man who checked tickets who would look the other way while we hid behind the cotton bales on the boat's deck. He'd pass us food throughout the journey and he'd knock three times when it was safe to disembark.

"You're going to be afraid, but whatever you do, don't show it," Jupiter said. "Imagine what it would be like to walk through that square on free legs; fix your eyes to the heavens and walk forward, one step at a time, but also like you're already there, like you already made it and you're looking back, showing somebody the route you took to get there."

We stopped to eat the rest of the vegetables and corn patties, raw fish Jupiter had caught that we ripped apart in chunks.

"We're almost there," my daddy said while he ate. He was getting nervous, I could see that in the way his eyes wouldn't settle on mine, and he kept looking toward the water in disbelief, like any minute he might glance up and realize he had imagined the whole journey.

"We're not almost there. We are there. We're not going there. We arrived. I told you that." Jupiter spit out a bone behind him.

341

Daddy nodded. "You're right, you're right," he said. "Let me ask you something. How'd you get that white man to believe you, not just that, to accept what you said?"

"Domingo," Jupiter started.

Mama's eyes drifted over toward him while he spoke.

"People carry messages on their faces. They speak their intentions toward you in that way. It's how you know if a woman means you harm or good, if she's going to let you have her; it's how you know how much cane is going to be enough for the day without the overseer saying one word; it's how we survive. I looked at that man this morning and I knew I could bend him; he had a story inside him that made it easy for me to make him see the world through my eyes." Jupiter paused. "But not every white man is like that. You should know. If we get caught again, and I don't start talking, run. That means there's nothing I can do." He looked away toward the river. "That means our power is going to come from running."

After we ate, we covered another mile. We could see the Cabildo and the cathedral's three steeples. The women had warned us we would need to pass them to reach the dock. *The square won't be busy at night,* they'd said, *but come morning, you'll find open brothels and bars, slave markets. You'll want to pick the exact moment so you're not tarrying too long in the light, but you don't want to miss that boat when it leaves either.*

Now it was time to change clothes.

We were covered in mud, our arms and legs cut from tree branches. The sun wasn't quite up but it was rising. If we walked to the dock now, we'd have to wait in the open, hope we blended in with the firemen and deckhands. If we stayed here, we'd risk being found lurking.

"Not yet," Jupiter said. "My spirit is telling me, not yet."

Mama pulled me to her, sat me in her lap. She kissed me more than once, all over my face, and she rubbed my back up and down like she was trying to push something inside me I might absorb.

Jupiter looked at her with an odd expression on his face, like he was seeing something for the first time.

"That's enough of that," he said, and he pulled me off of her.

That was when we heard the dogs' yelps. I looked up and saw in the distance two men on horseback followed by a band of hounds. Jupiter yanked me up by my neckline. Before I knew what had happened, we were running, Mommy and Daddy behind me, the men behind them. The dogs' growls grew closer. There was a great gulf growing between me and Jupiter and Mama and Daddy. I wanted to tell him to wait for them. I wanted to tell him there wasn't anywhere worth going if they wouldn't be there beside me, but at every step, I felt the tap of his knee against my chest, and I wrapped my arms around his neck, slick with sweat. I alternated between looking ahead at the ships and my mama and daddy behind me, struggling to keep up. I had just turned back when a rope swung out and caught Daddy. I saw his leg buckle under him. Mama fell on top of him and moaned. Jupiter looked back, raised his left arm, and fired three shots into the air, then he lifted me higher, flying more than walking, sliding the gun into his pocket. I rammed my small fists into his chest, then I reached my hands out to my mama, cried for her too, but she stayed put beside Daddy.

"Go," I heard her scream. "Go on now."

"Those the slaves belong to Tom Dufrene," one of the catchers said.

"Go on now," my mother repeated, and I thought I heard her laugh.

AVA

I leave Martha's for good, and I head straight for my mother's. I'm inside, rehashing my escape, when her phone rings. I can hear from her side of the conversation that it's Hazel.

"How far apart are they? Well, what's wrong with his car? All right, all right, I'll be there in an hour. Let me just get myself together." And then before she hangs up, "You got this, girl, okay? You got this."

She heads to her bedroom to pack her bag: a journal, lavender lotion, sage oils, heating pads, a copy of Hazel's birth plan, and affirmations the girl had written on index cards.

"I could use you," she says as she stuffs her bag full. "The thing is, her boyfriend isn't going to make it after all. She has aunties and cousins but they moved to Baton Rouge after the storm. You don't have

345

to stay the whole time, just the early part before we head to the hospital. The first stages of labor could last hours."

"I'm in," I say, almost embarrassed at how excited I am to be joining. "I'm not taking care of Martha," I add. "I don't have anything else to do."

We stand at Hazel's door for some time after we ring the bell. When she finally opens it, she's clutching the base of her stomach.

"That was a bad one," she says.

"Yeah, it's going to be like that for a while," my mother says back.

She walks in and starts to work: clearing space in the living room, laying quilts and blankets onto the floor, guiding Hazel to positions that might take the pressure off, all fours, then on her side. Before we'd come, I'd watched my mother fill socks with rice. She heats them now, as Hazel bends with another contraction, and presses them against Hazel's back.

"It's just energy," she says when the pain has ebbed. "It's all just energy," she repeats. "Our job is to diffuse it. Rock it out. Sing it out. You'll know the best way to move, the best way to let the pain out. Some people want to grunt, but that just traps the pressure inside. No, it's more of an exhale."

There's quiet as we wait, and my mother closes her eyes and presses her hands to the ceiling, palms up.

Mother God, Yemaya, Spirit World,
   Guides, and Ancestors,
We call on you today to show us the old
   ways.
We know there's nothing new under the
   sun, and we ask you to
Fill our minds with ancient wisdom, our
   hearts with intuition.
Take our hands, order our words,
So you are the one touching Hazel,
   hollowing out her pain,
So you are the one directing her
   thoughts, opening her heart to peace.
Center Hazel's mind in the present
   moment.

"Yes, Lord," I call out, without meaning to.

Show her how you create a new thing, a
   new moment, new life
In the magic folds of your own womb.
Let her lean on you,
Settle her heart with thanksgiving.
Be with us tonight and always,
Amen.

"Amen," I repeat.

Before I open my eyes, Hazel screams. My mother hurries over and takes her hand. She kneels down on all fours, swaying from side to side, and Hazel follows her, awkward at first, but as the pain deepens, her body loosens. She closes her eyes and groans.

"Good," my mother says. "Good," and she makes the sound with her. "Let the pain guide the exhale," she says. "Let it find the chord that's going to match it. Let it find the chord that's going to bring it home."

As they're talking, a voice tells me to run a bath. I fill the tub with warm water, walk back into the living room, and sit on the other side of my mother, rubbing Hazel's back up and down. It's not just her back but the top of her legs that seems to be calling for attention. Watching her writhe has awakened something in me, a memory of that steep throb that preceded King's birth, the one I never thought I would overcome. And it's not just memory because it's based on what's in front of me, like a part of my body corresponds with Hazel's, and I know before she sits up and says the contraction is over that the pain has ebbed, for now.

"Next time, let's go straight to the tub," I say. "It's getting to that point," and I surprise myself with my own authority.

My mother looks over at me with a smile and says, "All right."

Variations of the same unfold over the rest of the night. Hazel has quiet spurts where she's joking about the old-school music my mama is playing: Dinah Washington and Ella Fitzgerald.

"This sounds like this was recorded in like 1492 or something."

But she always braces up right before the contraction hits. I lead her back and forth from the tub, guide her to a kneel; I knead the base of her back with my fists, squeeze her hips together. I feel awkward at first but I know the scale of moan that needs to be expelled to soothe her, and I model the sound so she won't feel funny making it alone in her house, and I get on all fours with her, rocking my hips and groaning so the pain isn't trapped inside her body but given a channel to follow out.

By midnight, Hazel is ready to go to the hospital. I sit in the back with her while Mama drives.

When we arrive, the nurses lead Hazel to a room, examine her, and find she's eight centimeters dilated. My mother leaves with them to look for a doctor. As comfortable as I've become with this process, I'm nervous being alone with her. The pain has spiked, so has her terror, and the methods I've tried seem to be waning in usefulness. She's sitting on a birthing ball now, leaning against the hospital bed for support, and I'm squatting behind her, pressing into her back with my palms.

I can see from the monitor that there's another contraction coming.

"It's okay," I say. "It's going to be okay."

She closes her eyes and sways and groans through it. When she's done, she turns to me. "I can't do this anymore. It's even worse than last time, and you see how that turned out."

"You're so close," I say. "You can't give up now. In less than an hour, you're going to be a mother."

"That's what they said before," she says, and she starts to cry. "I was so geared up for it, I was so ready, and then —" she holds her face in her hands. "And then nothing."

"That was last time," I say, "but it's different now. You have to accept it's possible that things are going to be different now."

She shakes her head.

"You can use it though," I say. "All the pain, the disappointment, the anger, let it give you strength, let it give you power."

"I just want it to be over," she says.

And I feel like the same force that had

350

been moving my hands earlier today, guiding them up and down her back, squeezing her hips, telling me what temperature to run the water, is there again, directing the flow of my words, lending them a confidence they wouldn't have possessed on their own.

"I'm going to be here with you today," I say. "Where you don't have the strength, I'm going to give you mine, let you stand on it. I'm going to sit here with you and see it through."

That seems to calm her. The doctor comes in, my mother trailing her, and we help Hazel back onto the bed.

The doctor reaches inside her, then tells her she's ready to push.

"Can you give me one big one?" she asks.

And Hazel nods through a contraction.

I lean down to whisper in her ear, more a chant than a sentence, "All the women who came before you are standing beside you and they're cheering you on, they're guiding you to the finish." My eyes are closed as I talk, and I can see Josephine standing in her farm, just like the picture. This time, she's holding two children's hands in hers, a girl around the age of five and a much older boy, and they're all gazing at me with expectant eyes.

"Good girl," the doctor says. "Very good."

I can see the baby's head's out, slick and black.

"One more," the doctor says, "you got one more push in you, Hazel," and she grunts.

I keep talking.

"This is it, everything you've been preparing for, and it's already done; it became yours when you rose up to meet it."

She pushes again, and the baby is all the way out, quiet at first, but then he lets out an undeniable wail, and Hazel joins him.

"You did it," my mother screams. "You did it."

"I did it," Hazel repeats. "I did it."

The nurse lays the baby on her chest and he stops crying. He has thin skin the same peach color King was and I am taken aback for a minute. I close my eyes to say a prayer, and Josephine is there again, still holding the children's hands but looking elsewhere.

Hazel turns to me. "I couldn't have done it without you," she says. She looks down at the baby now, kissing the top of his head, and he squeezes her index finger in his fist. "You couldn't have told me today was going to go any different than it went last time," she goes on. "I really couldn't see it. But it's like another world opened up for me. I'm telling you, I don't feel like it's the same world."

■ ■ ■ ■

Hazel's aunties and cousins make it in, so after my mother helps the baby latch, we head back home. King is waiting for us there, and when I walk in, he rushes into my arms.

"You're in a good mood," I say.

He shrugs, trying to play it cool. I tell him about the baby.

"He reminded me of you, coming out. I can still see you in my arms. I could hold you in the palm of one hand."

"We're going to be here for a minute," I say, sitting down, "while I get myself together. I'm sorry about that."

He shakes his head. "I'm not. A change will be good."

He kisses me, then heads upstairs. My mother joins me on the sofa.

"You really came to life tonight, huh? I hate to say *I told you so.* You know I hate to say it."

"You were right," I say. "You were right."

She nods and smiles, places her hand over mine.

"How are you feeling otherwise?" she asks.

"Bittersweet," I say.

In the car, my father had called and told

me the hospital was going to admit my grandmother. She'll likely go to a facility when she's released. A nice one, he'd stressed, and I know that is best, but I'm sad for her too. Still Hazel had said she felt like another world had opened up, and in that world she was going to be allowed to keep her baby. I could see a new world opening for me too, and there's no room for guilt in this one.

I remember Josephine. I close my eyes, and she's not as vivid as she had been earlier, but still close enough that I know I didn't imagine her. She's settled in for the night, her hands folded beneath her face, a blue scarf wrapped tight around her head, a cluster of stones circling her pillow. Her eyes are closed but she is smiling. She seems so pleased with herself.

ACKNOWLEDGMENTS

My editor, Jack Shoemaker, enhances my vision and grounds it in the page. My agent, Michael Carlisle, is an advocate and friend. Jane Vandenburgh makes me and my work better. Megan Fishmann and Jenn Kovitz are pillars of knowledge and support. Jennifer Alton, Dory Athey, Katie Boland, Nicole Caputo, Jordan Koluch, Miyako Singer, Yukiko Tominaga, and everyone at Counterpoint and Catapult who has had a hand in this project — you are magicians, and it is awesome to behold. Jaya Miceli, the cover is perfect.

I am indebted to the following books: *Chained to the Land: Voices from Cotton & Cane Plantations* by Lynette Ater Tanner; *Rise and Fly: Tall Tales and Mostly True Rules of Bid Whist* by Greg Morrison and Yanick Rice Lamb; *American Uprising: The Untold Story of America's Largest Slave Revolt* by Daniel Rasmussen; *To 'Joy My Freedom:*

Southern Black Women's Lives and Labors after the Civil War by Tera W. Hunter; *Back Through the Veil: A Brief History of African-Americans Living in Mansura, (Volume 1)* by Donald G. Prier, PhD; *Slave Escapes & the Underground Railroad in North Carolina* by Steve M. Miller and J. Timothy Allen; *Freedom's Women: Black Women and Families in Civil War Era Mississippi* by Noralee Frankel; *Jambalaya: The Natural Woman's Book of Personal Charms and Practical Rituals* by Luisah Teish; *Mammon & Manon Early New Orleans: First Slave Society* by Thomas N. Ingersoll; *Twelve Years a Slave* by Solomon Northup; *The Way of the Elders: Western African Spirituality & Tradition* by Adama Doumbia and Naomi Doumbia; *Motherwit: An Alabama Midwife's Story* by Onnie Lee Logan and Katherine Clark; *Slave Religion: The "Invisible Institution" in the Antebellum South* by Albert J. Raboteau; *American Negro Songs: 230 Folk Songs and Spirituals, Religious and Secular* by John W. Work; *Africans in Colonial Louisiana: The Development of Afro-Creole Culture in the Eighteenth Century* by Gwendolyn Midlo Hall; *Freedom Colonies: Independent Black Texans in the Time of Jim Crow* by James H. Conrad, Thad Sitton, and Richard Orton; *Sharecropping in*

North Louisiana: A Family's Struggle Through the Great Depression by Lillian Laird Duff and Linda Duff Niemeir; *Slave Culture: Nationalist Theory and the Foundations of Black America* by Sterling Stuckey; *Freedom After Slavery: The Black Experience and the Freedmen's Bureau in Reconstruction Texas* by Lavonne Jackson Leslie, PhD; *Slavery's Exiles: The Story of the American Maroons* by Sylviane A. Diouf; *Mississippi Slave Narratives: A Folk History of Slavery in the United States from Interviews with Former Mississippi Slaves* by Federal Works Project; *The Underground Railroad from Slavery to Freedom: A Comprehensive History* by Wilbur H. Siebert; *Eight, True, Short Stories of Daring Slave Escapes: Tales From the Underground Railroad* by Julie McDonald; *Delivered by Midwives: African American Midwifery in the Twentieth-Century South* by Jenny M. Luke; *The Underground Railroad: Authentic Narratives and First-Hand Accounts* by William Still and Ian Finseth; *Slavery by Another Name: The Re-Enslavement of Black Americans from the Civil War to World War II* by Douglas A. Blackmon; *Harriet Tubman: The Road to Freedom* by Catherine Clinton; *What Love Can Do: Recollected Stories of Slavery and Freedom in New Orleans and the*

Surrounding Area by Arthur Mitchell and Gayle Nolan; *New Orleans after the Civil War: Race, Politics, and a New Birth of Freedom* by Justin A. Nystrom; *Seven African Powers: The Orishas* by Monique Joiner Siedlak; *Trouble in Mind: Black Southerners in the Age of Jim Crow* by Leon F. Litwack; *The World That Made New Orleans: From Spanish Silver to Congo Square* by Ned Sublette.

Thank you, Blane Clayton, Crystal Tenille Irby, Jamie Kennedy, and Debhora Singleton for your doula, bid whist, New Orleans, and life jewels.

Kathryn Kefauver and Leta McCollough Seletzky, your edits are indispensable and so is your encouragement.

Anisse Gross, Rachel Khong, Lydia Kiesling, Reese Kwon, Caille Millner, Andi Mudd, Esmé Weijun Wang, and Colin Winette, it has been an honor.

I am deeply grateful to Allysia Adams, Lucy Alvarez, Melinda Bowman, Katherine Williams Brinkman, Chanda McGhee, Vanessa Motley, Meredith Robinson, Erin Shelton, LJ Smith, Betsy Sexton, Carlton Sexton, Nubia Solomon, Iris Tate, Johanna Thomas, Kathryn Washington, Josie Wilkerson, Patsy Wilkerson, Felthus Wilkerson Jr., Bruce Williams, Trevor Williams, and so many others for holding me up this year.

My mother is a creative genius. I'm just glad she passed some down.

Chuckie, becoming a founding member of TFC has been my greatest joy and honor.

Nina, Carter, and Miles, may you always know you are loved beyond measure; may you always remember you are ten thousand strong.

ABOUT THE AUTHOR

Margaret Wilkerson Sexton, born and raised in New Orleans, studied creative writing at Dartmouth College and law at UC Berkeley. Her debut novel, *A Kind of Freedom,* was long-listed for the National Book Award and the Northern California Book Award, won the Crook's Corner Book Prize, and was the recipient of the First Novelist Award from the Black Caucus of the American Library Association. She lives in the San Francisco Bay Area with her family. Find out more at margaretwilkerson sexton.com.

Margaret Wilkerson Sexton, born and raised in New Orleans, studied creative writing at Dartmouth College and law at UC Berkeley. Her debut novel, A Kind of Freedom, was long-listed for the National Book Award and the Northern California Book Award, won the Crook's Corner Book Prize, and was the recipient of the First Novelist Award from the Black Caucus of the American Library Association. She lives in the San Francisco Bay Area with her family. Find out more at margaretwilkerson sexton.com.

The employees of Thorndike Press hope you have enjoyed this Large Print book. All our Thorndike, Wheeler, and Kennebec Large Print titles are designed for easy reading, and all our books are made to last. Other Thorndike Press Large Print books are available at your library, through selected bookstores, or directly from us.

For information about titles, please call:
(800) 223-1244

or visit our website at:
gale.com/thorndike

To share your comments, please write:

Publisher
Thorndike Press
10 Water St., Suite 310
Waterville, ME 04901